MAF

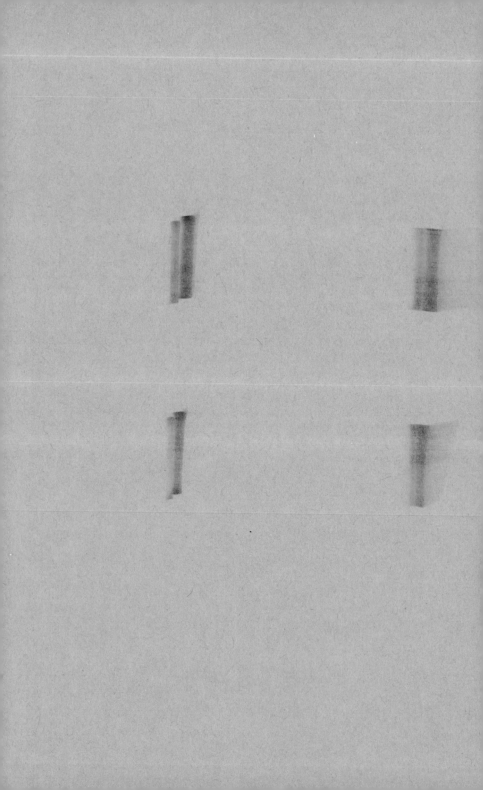

THE NATURALS

JENNIFER LYNN BARNES

HYPERION | *New York*

Printed in the United States of America
First Edition
10 9 8 7 6 5 4 3 2 1
G475-5664-5-13227

Library of Congress Cataloging-in-Publication Data
Barnes, Jennifer (Jennifer Lynn)
  The Naturals / Jennifer Lynn Barnes.
    pages cm
  Summary: "Seventeen-year-old Cassie, who has a natural ability to read
people, joins an elite group of criminal profilers at the FBI in order to help
solve cold cases"—Provided by publisher.
  ISBN 978-1-4231-6823-2 (hardback)—ISBN 1-4231-6823-2
[1. Criminal profilers—Fiction. 2. Criminal investigation—Fiction. 3. United
States. Federal Bureau of Investigation—Fiction. 4. Mystery and detective
stories.] I. Title.
  PZ7.B26225Nat 2013
  [Fic]—dc23   2013022685

Designed by Abby Kuperstock
Text is set in 12-point Fairfield Light LH.

Visit www.un-requiredreading.com

THE NATURALS

*For Neha, who understands the human mind and
uses her powers for good, not evil (mostly)*

THE NATURALS

PART ONE:
KNOWING

YOU

You've chosen and chosen well. Maybe this one will be the one who stops you. Maybe she'll be different. Maybe she'll be enough.

The only thing that is certain is that she's special.

You think it's her eyes—not the color: an icy, see-through blue. Not the lashes, or the shape, or the way she doesn't need eyeliner to give them the appearance of a cat's.

No, it's what's behind those icy blues that brings the audience out in droves. You feel it, every time you look at her. The certainty. The knowing. That otherworldly glint she uses to convince people that she's the real deal.

Maybe she is.

Maybe she really can see things. Maybe she knows things. Maybe she's everything she claims to be and more. But watching her, counting her breaths, you smile, because deep down, you know that she isn't going to stop you.

You don't really want her to stop you.

She's fragile.

Perfect.

Marked.

And the one thing this so-called psychic won't see coming is you.

CHAPTER 1

The hours were bad. The tips were worse, and the majority of my coworkers definitely left something to be desired, but *c'est la vie, que será será,* insert foreign language cliché of your choice here. It was a summer job, and that kept Nonna off my back. It also prevented my various aunts, uncles, and kitchen-sink cousins from feeling like they had to offer me temporary employment in their restaurant/butcher shop/legal practice/boutique. Given the size of my father's very large, very extended (and very Italian) family, the possibilities were endless, but it was always a variation on the same theme.

My dad lived half a world away. My mother was missing, presumed dead. I was everyone's problem and nobody's.

Teenager, presumed troubled.

"Order up!"

With practiced ease, I grabbed a plate of pancakes (side

of bacon) with my left hand and a two-handed breakfast burrito (jalapeños on the side) with my right. If the SATs didn't go well in the fall, I had a real future ahead of me in the crappy diner industry.

"Pancakes with a side of bacon. Breakfast burrito, jalapeños on the side." I slid the plates onto the table. "Anything else I can get for you gentlemen?"

Before either of them opened their mouths, I knew exactly what these two were going to say. The guy on the left was going to ask for extra butter. And the guy on the right? He was going to need another glass of water before he could even *think* about those jalapeños.

Ten-to-one odds, he didn't even like them.

Guys who actually liked jalapeños didn't order them on the side. Mr. Breakfast Burrito just didn't want people to think he was a wuss—only the word he would have used wasn't *wuss*.

Whoa there, Cassie, I told myself sternly. *Let's keep it PG.*

As a general rule, I didn't curse much, but I had a bad habit of picking up on other people's quirks. Put me in a room with a bunch of English people, and I'd walk out with a British accent. It wasn't intentional—I'd just spent a lot of time over the years getting inside other people's heads.

Occupational hazard. Not mine. My mother's.

"Could I get a few more of these butter packets?" the guy on the left asked.

I nodded—and waited.

"More water," the guy on the right grunted. He puffed out his chest and ogled my boobs.

I forced a smile. "I'll be right back with that water." I managed to keep from adding *pervert* to the end of that sentence, but only just.

I was still holding out hope that a guy in his late twenties who pretended to like spicy food and made a point of staring at his teenage waitress's chest like he was training for the Ogling Olympics might be equally showy when it came to leaving tips.

Then again, I thought as I went for refills, *he might turn out to be the kind of guy who stiffs the little bitty waitress just to prove he can.*

Absentmindedly, I turned the details of the situation over in my mind: the way that Mr. Breakfast Burrito was dressed; his likely occupation; the fact that his friend, who'd ordered the pancakes, was wearing a much more expensive watch.

He'll fight to grab the check, then tip like crap.

I hoped I was wrong—but was fairly certain that I wasn't.

Other kids spent their preschool years singing their way through the ABCs. I grew up learning a different alphabet. Behavior, personality, environment—my mother called them the BPEs, and they were the tricks of her trade. Thinking that way wasn't the kind of thing you could just turn off—not even once you were old enough to understand that when your mother told people she was psychic, she was *lying*, and when she took their money, it was *fraud*.

Even now that she was gone, I couldn't keep from figuring people out, any more than I could give up breathing, blinking, or counting down the days until I turned eighteen.

"Table for one?" A low, amused voice jostled me back into reality. The voice's owner looked like the type of boy who would have been more at home in a country club than a diner. His skin was perfect, his hair artfully mussed. Even though he phrased his words like they were a question, they weren't—not really.

"Sure," I said, grabbing a menu. "Right this way."

A closer observation told me that Country Club was about my age. A smirk played across his perfect features, and he walked with the swagger of high school nobility. Just looking at him made me feel like a serf.

"This okay?" I asked, leading him to a table near the window.

"This is fine," he said, slipping into the chair. Casually, he surveyed the room with bulletproof confidence. "You get a lot of traffic in here on weekends?"

"Sure," I replied. I was starting to wonder if I'd lost the ability to speak in complex sentences. From the look on the boy's face, he probably was, too. "I'll give you a minute to look over the menu."

He didn't respond, and I spent my minute bringing Pancakes and Breakfast Burrito their checks, plural. I figured that if I split it in half, I might end up with half a decent tip.

"I'll be your cashier whenever you're ready," I said, fake smile firmly in place.

I turned back toward the kitchen and caught the boy by the window watching me. It wasn't an *I'm ready to order* stare. I wasn't sure what it was, actually—but every bone in my body told me it was *something*. The niggling sensation that there was a key detail that I was missing about this whole situation—about *him*—wouldn't go away. Boys like that didn't usually eat in places like this.

They didn't stare at girls like me.

Self-conscious and wary, I crossed the room.

"Did you decide what you'd like?" I asked. There was no getting out of taking his order, so I let my hair fall in my face, obscuring his view of it.

"Three eggs," he said, hazel eyes fixed on what he could see of mine. "Side of pancakes. Side of ham."

I didn't need to write the order down, but I suddenly found myself wishing for a pen, just so I'd have something to hold on to. "What kind of eggs?" I asked.

"You tell me." The boy's words caught me off guard.

"Excuse me?"

"Guess," he said.

I stared at him through the wisps of hair still covering my face. "You want me to guess how you want your eggs cooked?"

He smiled. "Why not?"

And just like that, the gauntlet was thrown.

"Not scrambled," I said, thinking out loud. Scrambled eggs were too average, too common, and this was a guy who liked to be a little bit different. Not too different, though, which ruled out poached—at least in a place like this. Sunny-side up would have been too messy for him; over hard wouldn't be messy enough.

"Over easy." I was as sure of the conclusion as I was of the color of his eyes. He smiled and closed his menu.

"Are you going to tell me if I was right?" I asked—not because I needed confirmation, but because I wanted to see how he would respond.

The boy shrugged. "Now, where would the fun be in that?"

I wanted to stay there, staring, until I figured him out, but I didn't. I put his order in. I delivered his food. The lunch rush snuck up on me, and by the time I went back to check on him, the boy by the window was gone. He hadn't even waited for his check—he'd just left twenty dollars on the table. I had just about decided that he could make me play guessing games to his heart's content for a twelve-dollar tip when I noticed the bill wasn't the only thing he'd left.

There was also a business card.

I picked it up. Stark white. Black letters. Evenly spaced. There was a seal in the upper left-hand corner, but relatively little text: a name, a job title, a phone number. Across the top of the card, there were four words, four little words that knocked the wind out of me as effectively as a jab to the chest.

I pocketed the card—and the tip. I went back to the kitchen. I caught my breath. And then I looked at it again.

Tanner Briggs. The name.

Special Agent. Job title.

Federal Bureau of Investigation.

Four words, but I stared at them so hard that my vision blurred and I could only make out three letters.

What in the world had I done to attract the attention of the FBI?

fter an eight-hour shift, my body was bone tired, but my mind was whirring. I wanted to shut myself in my room, collapse on my bed, and figure out what the Hello Kitty had happened that afternoon.

Unfortunately, it was Sunday.

"There she is! Cassie, we were just about to send the boys out looking for you." My aunt Tasha was among the more reasonable of my father's various siblings, so she didn't wink and ask me if I'd found myself a boyfriend to occupy my time.

That was Uncle Rio's job. "Our little heartbreaker, eh? You out there breaking hearts? Of course she is!"

I'd been a regular fixture at Sunday night dinners ever since Social Services had dropped me off on my father's doorstep—metaphorically, thank God—when I was twelve. After five years, I still hadn't ever heard Uncle Rio ask a question that he did not immediately proceed to answer himself.

"I don't have a boyfriend," I said. This was a well-established script, and that was my line. "Promise."

"What are we talking about?" one of Uncle Rio's sons asked, plopping himself down on the living room sofa, dangling his legs over the side.

"Cassie's boyfriend," Uncle Rio replied.

I rolled my eyes. "I don't *have* a boyfriend."

"Cassie's secret boyfriend," Uncle Rio amended.

"I think you have me confused with Sofia and Kate," I said. Under normal circumstances I wouldn't have thrown any of my female cousins under the bus, but desperate times called for desperate measures. "They're far more likely to have secret boyfriends than I am."

"Bah," Uncle Rio said. "Sofia's boyfriends are never secret."

And on it went—good-natured ribbing, family jokes. I played the part, letting their energy infect me, saying what they wanted me to say, smiling the smiles they wanted to see. It was warm and safe and happy—but it wasn't me.

It never was.

As soon as I was sure I wouldn't be missed, I ducked into the kitchen.

"Cassandra. Good." My grandmother, elbow-deep in flour, her gray hair pulled into a loose bun at the nape of her neck, gave me a warm smile. "How was work?"

Despite her little-old-lady appearance, Nonna ruled the entire family like a general directing her troops. Right now, I was the one drifting out of formation.

"Work was work," I said. "Not bad."

"But not good, either?" She narrowed her eyes.

If I didn't play this right, I'd have ten job offers within the hour. Family took care of family—even when "family" was perfectly capable of taking care of herself.

"Today was actually decent," I said, trying to sound cheerful. "Someone left me a twelve-dollar tip."

And also, I added silently, *a business card from the FBI.*

"Good," Nonna said. "That is good. You had a good day."

"Yeah, Nonna," I said, crossing the room to kiss her cheek, because I knew it would make her happy. "It was a good day."

By the time everyone cleared out at nine, the card felt like lead in my pocket. I tried to help Nonna with the dishes, but she shooed me upstairs. In the quiet of my own room, I could feel the energy draining out of me, like air out of a slowly wilting balloon.

I sat down on my bed and then let myself fall backward. The old springs groaned with the impact, and I closed my eyes. My right hand found its way to my pocket, and I pulled out the card.

It was a joke. It had to be. That was why the pretty,

country-club boy had felt *off* to me. That was why he'd taken an interest—to mock me.

But he didn't really seem the type.

I opened my eyes and looked at the card. This time, I let myself read it out loud. "Special Agent Tanner Briggs. Federal Bureau of Investigation."

A few hours in my pocket hadn't changed the text on the card. FBI? Seriously? Who was this guy trying to kid? He'd looked sixteen, seventeen, max.

Not like a special agent.

Just special. I couldn't push that thought down, and my eyes flitted reflexively toward the mirror on my wall. It was one of the great ironies of my life that I'd inherited all of my mother's features, but none of the magic with which they'd come together on her face. She'd been beautiful. I was odd—odd-looking, oddly quiet, always the odd one out.

Even after five years, I still couldn't think of my mother without thinking of the last time I'd seen her, shooing me out of her dressing room, a wide smile on her face. Then I thought about coming back to the dressing room. About the blood—on the floor, on the walls, on the mirror. I hadn't been gone long. I'd opened the door—

"Snap out of it," I told myself. I sat up and pushed my back up against the headboard, unable to quit thinking about the smell of blood and that moment of knowing it was my mother's and praying it wasn't.

What if *that* was what this was about? What if the card wasn't a joke? What if the FBI was looking into my mother's murder?

It's been five years, I told myself. But the case was still open. My mother's body had never been found. Based on the amount of blood, that was what the police had been looking for from the beginning.

A body.

I turned the business card over in my hands. On the back, there was a handwritten note.

Cassandra, it said, PLEASE CALL.

That was it. My name, and then the directive to call, in capital letters. No explanation. No nothing.

Below those words, someone else had scribbled a second set of instructions in small, sharp letters—barely readable. I traced my finger over the letters and thought about the boy from the diner.

Maybe he wasn't the special agent.

So that makes him what? The messenger?

I didn't have an answer, but the words scrawled across the bottom of the card stood out to me, every bit as much as Special Agent Tanner Briggs's *PLEASE CALL.*

If I were you, I wouldn't.

YOU

You're good at waiting. Waiting for the right moment. Waiting for the right girl. You have her now, and still, you're waiting. Waiting for her to wake up. Waiting for her to open those eyes and see you.

Waiting for her to scream.

And scream.

And scream.

And realize that no one can hear her but you.

You know how this will go, how she'll be angry, then scared, then swear up and down that if you let her go, she won't tell a soul. She'll lie to you, and she'll try to manipulate you, and you'll have to show her—the way you've showed so many others—how that just won't do.

But not yet. Right now, she's still sleeping. Beautiful—but not as beautiful as she will be when you're done.

CHAPTER 3

It took me two days, but I called the number. Of course I did, because even though there was a 99 percent chance this was some kind of hoax, there was a 1 percent chance that it wasn't.

I didn't realize I was holding my breath until someone picked up.

"This is Briggs."

I couldn't pinpoint what was more disarming—the fact that this "Agent Briggs" had apparently given me the number to his direct line or the way he answered the phone, like saying "hello" would have been a waste of breath.

"Hello?" As if he could read my mind, Special Agent Tanner Briggs spoke again. "Anyone there?"

"This is Cassandra Hobbes," I said. "Cassie."

"Cassie." Something about the way Agent Briggs said my name made me think that he'd known before I'd said a single word that I didn't go by my full name. "I'm glad you called."

He waited for me to say something else, but I stayed silent. Everything you said or did was a data point you put out there in the world, and I didn't want to give this man any more information than I had to—not until I knew what he wanted from me.

"I'm sure you must be wondering why I contacted you— why I had Michael contact you."

Michael. So now the boy from the diner had a name.

"I have an offer I'd like you to consider."

"An offer?" It amazed me that my voice stayed every bit as calm and even as his.

"I believe this is a conversation best had in person, Ms. Hobbes. Is there somewhere you would be comfortable meeting?"

He knew what he was doing—letting me pick the location, because if he'd specified one, I might not have gone. I probably should have refused to meet with him anyway, but I couldn't, for the same reason that I'd had to pick up the phone and call.

Five years was a long time to go without a body. Without answers.

"Do you have an office?" I asked.

The slight pause on the other end of the phone told me that wasn't what he'd expected me to say. I could have asked him to meet me at the diner or a coffee shop near the high school or anywhere that I would have had the home court advantage, but I'd been taught to believe that there was no home court advantage.

You could tell more about a stranger by seeing their house than you ever would by inviting them to yours.

Besides, if this guy wasn't really an FBI agent, if he was some kind of pervert and this was some kind of game, I figured he'd probably have a heck of a time arranging a meeting at the local FBI office.

"I don't actually work out of Denver," he said finally. "But I'm sure I can set something up."

Probably not a pervert, then.

He gave me an address. I gave him a time.

"And Cassandra?"

I wondered what Agent Briggs hoped to accomplish by using my full first name. "Yes?"

"This isn't about your mother."

I went to the meeting anyway. Of course I did. Special Agent Tanner Briggs knew enough about me to know that my mother's case was the reason I'd followed the instructions on the card and called. I wanted to know how he'd come by that information, if he'd looked at her police file, if he *would* look at her file, provided I gave him whatever it was he wanted from me.

I wanted to know why Special Agent Tanner Briggs had made it his business to know about me, the same way a man shopping for a new computer might have memorized the specs of the model that had caught his eye.

"What floor?" The woman beside me in the elevator was in her early sixties. Her silvery blond hair was pulled back into a neat ponytail at the nape of her neck, and the suit she was wearing was perfectly tailored.

All business, just like Special Agent Tanner Briggs.

"Fifth floor," I said. "Please."

With nervous energy to burn, I snuck another glance at the woman and started piecing my way through her life story, as told by the way she was standing, her clothes, the faint accent in her speech, the clear coat of polish on her nails.

She was married.

No kids.

When she'd started in the FBI, it had been a boy's club.

Behavior. Personality. Environment. I could practically hear my mother coaching me through this impromptu analysis.

"Fifth floor." The woman's words were brisk, and I added another entry to my mental column—*impatient.*

Obligingly, I stepped out of the elevator. The door closed behind me, and I appraised my surroundings. It looked so . . . *normal.* If it hadn't been for the security checkpoint out front and the visitor's badge pinned to my faded black sundress, I never would have pegged this for a place devoted to fighting federal crime.

"So, what? You were expecting a dog-and-pony show?"

I recognized the voice instantly. The boy from the diner. *Michael.* He sounded amused, and when I turned to face him, there was a familiar smirk dancing its way through his features, one that he probably could have suppressed if he'd had the least inclination to try.

"I wasn't expecting anything," I told him. "I have no expectations."

He gave me a knowing look. "No expectations, no disappointments."

I couldn't tell if that was his appraisal of my current mental state or the motto by which he lived his own life. In fact, I was having trouble getting any handle on his personality at all. He'd traded his striped polo for a formfitting black T-shirt and his jeans for khaki slacks. He looked as out of place here as he had at the diner, like maybe that was the point.

"You know," he said conversationally, "I knew you'd come."

I raised an eyebrow at him. "Even though you told me not to?"

He shrugged. "My inner Boy Scout had to try."

If this guy had an inner Boy Scout, I had an inner flamingo.

"So, are you here to take me to Special Agent Tanner Briggs?" I asked. The words came out curtly, but at least I didn't sound fascinated, infatuated, or even the least bit drawn to the sound of his voice.

"Hmmmmm." In response to my question, Michael made a noncommittal noise under his breath and inclined his head—as close to a yes as I was going to get. He led me around the bull pen and down a hallway. Neutral carpet, neutral walls, a neutral expression on his criminally handsome face.

"So what does Briggs have on you?" Michael asked. I could feel him watching me, looking for a surge of emotion—any emotion—to tell him if his question had hit a nerve.

It hadn't.

"You want me to be nervous about this," I told him, because that much was clear from his words. "And you told me not to come."

He smiled, but there was a hard glint to it, an edge. "I guess you could say I'm contrary."

I snorted. That was one word for it.

"Are you going to give me even a hint of what's going on here?" I asked as we neared the end of the hall.

He shrugged. "That depends. Are you going to stop playing Who's Got the Best Poker Face with me?"

That surprised a laugh out of me, and I realized that it had been a long time since I'd laughed because I couldn't help it and not because someone else was laughing, too.

Michael's smile lost its edge, and for a second, the expression utterly changed his face. If he'd been handsome before, he was beautiful now—but it didn't last. As quickly as the lightness had come, it faded.

"I meant what I wrote on that card," he said softly. He nodded to a closed office door to our right. "If I were you, I wouldn't go in there."

I knew then—the way I always knew things—that Michael had been in my shoes once and that he had opened the door. His warning was genuine, but I opened it, too.

"Ms. Hobbes. Please, come in."

With one last glance at Michael, I stepped into the room.

"Au revoir," the boy with the excellent poker face said, punctuating the words with an exaggerated flick of his fingers.

Special Agent Tanner Briggs cleared his throat. The door closed behind me. For better or worse, I was here to meet with an FBI agent. Alone.

"I'm glad you came, Cassie. Take a seat."

Agent Briggs was younger than I'd expected based on his phone voice. The gears in my brain turned slowly, incorporating his age into what I knew. An older man who took pains to appear businesslike was guarded. A twenty-nine-year-old who did the same wanted to be taken seriously.

There was a difference.

Obediently, I took a seat. Agent Briggs stayed in his chair, but leaned forward. The desk between us was clean, but for a stack of papers and two pens, one of which was missing its cap.

He wasn't naturally neat, then. For some reason, I found that comforting. He was ambitious, but not inflexible.

"Are you finished?" he asked me. His voice wasn't curt. If anything, he sounded genuinely curious.

"Finished with what?" I asked him.

"Analyzing me," he said. "I've only been in this office for two hours. I couldn't even guess what it is that has caught your attention, but I figured something would. With Naturals, something almost always does."

Naturals. He said the word like he was expecting me to repeat it with a question mark in my tone. I didn't say anything. The less I gave him, the more he'd show me.

"You're good at reading people, at taking little details and figuring out the big picture: who they are, what they want, how they operate." He smiled. "What kind of eggs they like."

"You invited me here because I'm good at guessing what kind of eggs people like?" I asked, unable to keep the incredulousness out of my voice.

He drummed his fingers over the desktop. "I asked you here because you have a natural aptitude for something that most people could spend a lifetime trying to learn."

I wondered if when he said *most people* he was referring at least in part to himself.

He took my continued silence as some kind of argument. "Are you telling me that you don't read people? That you can't tell me right now whether I'd rather play basketball or golf?"

Basketball. But he'd want people to think the answer was golf.

"You could try to explain to me how you figure things out, how you figure *people* out, Cassie, but the difference between you and the rest of the world is that to explain how you just figured out that I'd rather get a bloody nose on the basketball court than tee off with the boss, you'd have to backtrack. You'd have to sort out what the clues were and how you'd made sense of them, because you just do it. You don't even have to think about it, not the way that I would, not the way that my team would. You probably couldn't stop yourself if you tried."

I hadn't ever talked about this, not even with Mom, who'd taught me the parts of it that could be taught. People were people, but for better or worse, most days, they were just puzzles to me. Easy puzzles, hard puzzles, crosswords, mind-benders, sudoku. There was always an answer, and I couldn't stop myself from pushing until I found it.

"How do you know any of this?" I asked the man in front of me. "And even if it's true, even if I do have really good instincts about people, what's it to you?"

He leaned forward. "I know because I make it my business to know. Because I'm the one who convinced the FBI that they need to be looking for people like you."

"What do you want with me?"

He eased back in his chair. "What do you think I want with you, Cassie?"

My mouth went dry. "I'm seventeen."

"Natural aptitudes, like yours, peak in the teen years. Formal education, college, the wrong influences, could all interfere with the incredible raw potential you have now." He folded his hands neatly in front of him. "I want to see to it that you have the right influences, that your gift is molded into something extraordinary, something that you can use to do an incredible amount of good in this world."

Part of me wanted to laugh at him, to walk out of the room, to forget that any of this had ever happened, but the other part just kept thinking that for five years, I'd been living in limbo, like I was waiting for something without knowing what that something was.

"You can take as much time as you need to think about it, Cassie, but what I'm offering you is a once-in-a-lifetime chance. Our program is one of a kind, and it has the potential to turn Naturals—people like you—into something truly extraordinary."

"People like me," I repeated, my mind going ninety miles an hour. "And Michael."

The second part was a guess, but not much of one. In the two minutes we'd spent walking to this office, Michael had come closer to figuring out what was going on inside my head than anyone I'd ever met.

"And Michael." As he spoke, Agent Briggs's face became more animated. Gone was the hardened professional. This was personal. This program was something he believed in.

And he had something to prove.

"What would becoming a part of this program entail?" I asked, measuring his response. The enthusiasm on his face morphed into something far more intense. His eyes bored into mine.

"How would you feel about moving to Washington, DC?"

CHAPTER 4

How would I feel about moving to DC?

"I'm seventeen," I reiterated. "A better question might be how my legal guardians would feel about it."

"You wouldn't be the first minor I've recruited, Cassie. There are work-arounds."

Clearly, he had not met my Nonna.

"Five years ago, custody of Cassandra Hobbes was remitted to her biological father, one Vincent Battaglia, United States Air Force." Agent Briggs paused. "Fourteen months after your appearance in his life, your father was transferred overseas. You chose to remain here, with your paternal grandmother."

I didn't ask how Agent Briggs had come by that information. He was FBI. He probably knew what color toothbrush I used.

"My point, Cassie, is that legally, your father still has

custody, and I have every confidence that if you want this to happen, I can make it happen." Briggs paused again. "As far as the outside world is concerned, we're a gifted program. Very selective, with endorsements from some very important people. Your father is career military. He worries about the way you isolate yourself. That will make him easier to persuade than most."

I started to open my mouth to ask how exactly he'd determined that my father *worried*, but Briggs held up a hand.

"I don't walk into a situation like this blind, Cassie. Once you were flagged in the system as a potential recruit, I did my homework."

"Flagged?" I asked, raising my eyebrows. "For what?"

"I don't know. I wasn't the one who flagged you, and quite frankly, the details of your recruitment are moot unless you're interested in my offer. Say the word if you're not, and I'll leave Denver tonight."

I couldn't do that—and Agent Briggs probably knew it before he asked.

He picked up the capless pen and scrawled some notes on the edge of one of his papers. "If you have questions, you can ask Michael. I have no doubt he'll be painfully honest with you about his experience in the program so far." Briggs rolled his eyes heavenward in a gesture of exasperation so universal that I almost forgot about the badge and the suit. "And if there are any questions that I could answer for you . . ."

He trailed off and waited. I took the bait and started pressing him for details. Fifteen minutes later, my mind was reeling. The program—that was how he referred to it, again and again—was small, still in its trial stages. Their agenda was twofold: first, to educate those of us selected to participate and hone our natural skills, and second, to use those skills to aid the FBI from behind the scenes. I was free to leave the program at any time. I would be required to sign a nondisclosure agreement.

"There's one question you haven't asked, Cassie." Agent Briggs folded his hands in front of him again. "So I'll answer it for you. I know about your personal history. About your mother's case. And while I have no new information for you, I can say that after what you've been through, you have more reasons than most to want to do what we do."

"And what is that?" I asked, my throat tightening at the mere mention of the *m*-word. "You said that you'll provide training, and that in exchange I'll be consulting for you. Consulting on what, exactly? Training for what?"

He paused, but whether he was assessing me or adding emphasis to his answer, I wasn't sure.

"You'll be helping on cold cases. Ones the Bureau hasn't been able to close."

I thought of my mother—the blood on the mirror and the sirens and the way I used to sleep with a phone, hoping so desperately that it would ring. I had to force myself to keep breathing normally, to keep from closing my eyes and picturing my mom's impish, smiling face.

"What kind of cold cases?" I asked, my voice catching in my throat. My lips felt suddenly dry; my eyes felt wet.

Agent Briggs had the decency to ignore the emotion now evident on my face. "The exact assignments vary, depending on your specialty. Michael's a Natural at reading emotions, so he spends a great deal of time going over testimony and interrogation tapes. With his background, I suspect he'll ultimately be a good fit for our white-collar crime division, but a person with his skill set can be useful in any kind of investigation. One of the other recruits in the program is a walking encyclopedia who sees patterns and probabilities everywhere she looks. We started her out on crime scene analysis."

"And me?" I asked.

He was silent for a moment, measuring. I glanced at the papers on his desk and wondered if any of them were about me.

"You're a Natural profiler," he said finally. "You can look at a pattern of behavior and figure out the personality of the perpetrator, or guess how a given individual is likely to behave in the future. That tends to come in handy when we have a series of interrelated crimes, but no definite suspect."

I read in between the lines of that statement, but wanted to be sure. "Interrelated crimes?"

"Serial crimes," he said, choosing a different word and letting it hang in the air around us. "Abductions. Arson. Sexual assault." He paused, and I knew what the next word out of his mouth was going to be before he said it. "Murder."

The truth he'd been dancing around for the past hour was suddenly incredibly clear. He and his team, this program— they didn't just want to teach me how to hone my skills. They wanted to use them to catch killers.

Serial killers.

YOU

You look at the body and feel a rush of anger. Rage. It's supposed to be sublime. You're supposed to decide. You're supposed to feel the life go out of her. She isn't supposed to rush you.

She shouldn't be dead yet, but she is.

She should be perfect now, but she's not.

She didn't scream enough, and then she screamed too much, and she called you names. Names that He used to call you. And you got angry.

It was over too fast, too soon, and it wasn't your fault, damn it. It was hers. She's the one who made you angry. She's the one who ruined it.

You're better than this. You're supposed to be looking at her body and feeling the power, the rush. She's supposed to be a work of art.

But she's not.

You drive the knife into her stomach again and again, blinded to anything else. She's not perfect. She's not beautiful. She's nothing.

You're nothing.

But you won't stay nothing for long.

CHAPTER 5

I gave Agent Briggs the go-ahead to talk to my father. My father called me. Less than a week after I told my dad this was what I wanted, I got word that Briggs had obtained the necessary permissions. My paperwork had gone through. That night, I quit my job at the diner. I took a shower, changed into my pajamas, and prepared for World War III.

I was going to do this. I'd known that from almost the moment that Agent Briggs had started speaking. I cared about my grandmother. I did. And I knew how hard she and the rest of the family had tried to make me feel loved, no matter how I'd come to them or how much of my mother there was in me. But I'd never really belonged here. A part of me had never really left that fateful theater: the lights, the crowd, the blood. Maybe I never would, but Agent Briggs was offering me a chance to do something about it.

I might never solve my own mother's murder, but this program would turn me into the kind of person who could catch killers, who could make sure that another little girl, in another life, with another mother, would never have to see what I had seen.

It was morbid and horrifying and the very last life the family would have imagined for me—and I wanted it more than I had ever wanted anything.

I combed my fingers through my hair. Wet, it looked dark enough to pass for brown instead of auburn. The steam from the shower had brought some color into my cheeks. I looked like the type of girl who could belong here, with this family.

With wet hair, I didn't look so much like my mother.

"Chicken." I leveled the insult at my own reflection and then pushed back from the mirror. I could stay here until my hair dried—in fact, I could stay here until my hair went gray—and that wouldn't make the conversation I was about to have any easier.

Downstairs, Nonna was curled up in a recliner in the living room, reading glasses perched on her nose and a large-print romance novel open in her lap. She looked up the second I stepped in the room, her eagle eyes sharp.

"You are ready for bed early," she said, no small amount of suspicion in her voice. Nonna had successfully raised eight children. If I'd been the type to make trouble, there would have been none that I could have stirred up that she hadn't already seen.

"I quit my job today," I said, and the sparkle in her eyes told me those had been the wrong words to lead with. "I don't need you to get me a new one," I added hastily.

Nonna made a dismissive sound under her breath. "Of course not. You are *independent*. You do not need anything from your old Nonna. You do not care if she worries."

Well, this was going well.

"I don't want you to worry," I said, "but something's come up. An opportunity."

I'd already made the executive decision that Nonna didn't need to know what I'd be doing—or why. I stuck to the cover story that Agent Briggs had given me. "There's a school," I said. "A special program. The director came to see me last week."

Nonna harrumphed.

"He talked to Dad."

"The director of this program talked to your father," Nonna repeated. "And what did my son say to this man who could not be bothered to introduce himself to me?"

I explained as much as I could. I gave her a pamphlet that Agent Briggs had given me—one that didn't mention words like *profiling* or *serial killers* or *FBI*.

"It's a small program," I said. "At a kind of group home."

"And your father, he said you could go?" Nonna narrowed her eyes at the smiling kids on the front of the pamphlet, like they were personally responsible for leading her precious granddaughter astray.

"He already signed the papers, Nonna." I looked down at my hands, which had woven themselves together at my waist. "I'm going to go."

There was silence. Then a sharp intake of breath. And then an explosion.

I didn't speak Italian, but based on the emphatic gestures and the way she was spitting out the words, I was able to make an educated guess at a translation.

Nonna's granddaughter was moving cross-country to enroll in a government-sponsored gifted program over her dead and rotting corpse.

Nobody stages an intervention like my father's family stages an intervention. The Bat-Signal had nothing on the Battaglia-Signal, and less than twenty-four hours after Nonna sent out the distress call, the family had gathered in force. There was yelling and screaming and crying—and food. Lots of food. I was threatened and cajoled, browbeaten and clasped to multiple bosoms. But for the first time since I'd met this half of my family tree, I couldn't just temper my reactions to theirs. I couldn't give them what they wanted. I couldn't *pretend*.

The noise built to a crescendo, and I drew into myself and waited for it to pass. Eventually, they'd notice that I wasn't saying anything.

"Cassie, sweetheart, aren't you happy here?" one of my aunts asked finally. The rest of the table fell silent.

"I'm . . ." I couldn't say any more than that. I saw the realization pass over their faces. "It's not that I'm not happy," I interjected quickly. "It's just . . ."

For once, they heard what I *wasn't* saying. From the moment they'd learned of my existence, I'd been family to them. They hadn't realized that in my own eyes, I'd always been—and maybe always would be—an outsider.

"I need to do this," I said, my voice as quiet as theirs had been loud. "For my mom."

That was closer to the truth than I'd ever meant to tell them.

"You think your mother would have wanted you to do this?" Nonna asked. "To leave the family that loves you, that will take care of you, to go off to the other side of the country, alone, to do God knows what?"

It was meant as a rhetorical question, but I answered it: vehemently, decisively.

"Yes." I paused, expecting an argument, but I didn't get one. "I know you don't like it, and I hope you don't hate me for it, but I have to do this." I stood up. "I leave in three days. I'd really like to come back for Christmas, but if you don't want me here, I'd understand."

Nonna crossed the room in a second, surprisingly spry for someone her age. She poked a vicious finger into my chest. "You come home for Christmas," she said in a manner that made it quite clear she considered it an order. "You even think about not coming home?" She narrowed her eyes and drew her poking finger across her neck in a menacing fashion. *"Capisce?"*

A smile tugged at the edge of my lips, and tears burned in my eyes. *"Capisce."*

CHAPTER 6

Three days later, I left for the program. Michael was the one who came to pick me up. He parked out at the curb and waited.

"I do not like this," Nonna told me for maybe the thousandth time.

"I know." I brushed a kiss against her temple, and she cupped my head in her hands.

"You be good," she said fiercely. "You be careful. Your father," she added, as an afterthought. "I am going to kill him."

I glanced back over my shoulder and saw Michael standing with his back to a gleaming black Porsche. From a distance, I couldn't make out the expression on his face, but I had a suspicion that he wasn't having any trouble interpreting *my* feelings.

"I'll be careful," I told Nonna, turning my back on the boy with the discerning eye. "Promise."

"Eh," she said finally. "How much trouble can you get into? There are only a few students in the entire school."

A few students who were being trained to analyze crime scenes, pore over witness testimony, and track serial killers. What trouble could we possibly get into?

Without another word, I hauled my bag out to the car. Nonna followed and, when Michael opened the trunk but made no move to help me with my bag, she shot him a disapproving look.

"You are just going to stand there?" she asked.

With an almost imperceptible smirk, Michael took the bag from my hand and hoisted it effortlessly into the trunk. Then he leaned close, into my personal space, and whispered, "And here I'd pegged you as the kind of girl who'd want to do the heavy lifting herself."

Nonna eyed me. She eyed Michael. She eyed what little space there was between the two of us. And then she made a harrumphing sound.

"Anything happens to her," she told Michael, "this family—we know how to dispose of a body."

Instead of giving in to the mortification and burying my head in my hands, I said good-bye to Nonna and climbed into the car. Michael followed suit.

"Sorry about that," I said.

Michael arched one eyebrow. "About the death threat, or the imaginary chastity belt she's fitting you with as we speak?"

"Shut up."

"Oh, come on, Cassie. I think it's nice. You have a family that cares."

Maybe he thought that was nice, and maybe he didn't. "I don't want to talk about my family."

Michael grinned, completely undeterred. "I know."

I thought back to what Agent Briggs had told me about Michael's gift.

"You read emotions," I said.

"Facial expressions, posture, gestures, the works," he said. "You nibble on the inside of your lip when you're nervous. And you get this little wrinkle at the corner of your right eye when you're trying not to stare."

He said all of this without ever taking his eyes off the road. My gaze flitted to the speedometer, and I realized how fast we were going.

"Do you *want* to get pulled over?" I squeaked.

He shrugged. "You're the profiler," he said. "You tell me." He eased off the accelerator ever so slightly. "That's what profilers do, isn't it? You look at the way a person is dressed, or the way a person talks, every little detail, and you put that person in a box. You figure out what *kind* of individual you're dealing with, and you convince yourself that you know *exactly* what everyone else wants."

Okay, so he'd had an experience—and not a good one—with a profiler in the past. I took that to mean that the difficulty I'd been having getting a read on him was no accident. He *liked* keeping me guessing.

"You wear a different style of clothing every time I see you," I said. "You stand differently. You talk differently. You never say anything about yourself."

"Maybe I like being tall, dark, and mysterious," Michael replied, taking a turn so quickly that I had to remind myself to breathe.

"You're not that tall," I gritted out. He laughed.

"You're annoyed with me," he said, wiggling his eyebrows. "But also intrigued."

"Would you stop that?" I'd never realized how irritating it was to be the one under the microscope.

"I'll make you a deal," Michael said. "I'll stop trying to read your emotions if you stop trying to profile me."

I had so many questions—about the way he'd grown up, about his ability, about why he'd warned me to stay away—but unless I wanted him making an intense study of my emotions, I'd have to get my answers the normal way.

"Fine," I said. "Deal."

He smiled. "Excellent. Now, as a show of good faith, since

I've already spent a good chunk of time getting inside your head, I'll give you three questions to try to get inside mine."

The puzzle solver in me wanted to ask what kind of clothes he wore when there was no one around to see him, how many siblings he had, and which one of his parents had turned him into the kind of guy who was a little angry at the world.

But I didn't.

Anyone comfortable driving this fast wasn't going to shy away from a few little white lies. If I asked him what I wanted to know, all I would get was more mixed messages—so I asked him the only question I was fairly certain he'd answer honestly.

"What's with the Porsche?"

Michael took his eyes off the road just long enough to flick his gaze over to me, and I knew that I'd surprised him.

"The Porsche?" he repeated.

I nodded. "I'm pretty sure it's not standard FBI issue."

The edges of his lips curved upward, and for once, there was no dark undercurrent to the expression. "The Porsche was a present," he told me. "From my life before. Getting to keep it was one of the conditions I gave Briggs for joining up."

"Why wouldn't he have let you keep it?" I asked, realizing belatedly that I'd just burned question number two.

"Tax fraud," Michael replied. "Not mine. My father's."

From the tightness in his voice, I got the feeling that keeping the Porsche probably hadn't been the only condition of Michael's participation in the program. Whether he'd asked for the government to overlook his father's crimes or his father had bartered away his son in exchange for immunity, I wasn't sure.

I didn't ask.

Instead, I stuck to safer ground. "What's it like? The program?"

"I've only been there for a few months," Michael said. "Briggs sprung me to come get you. Good behavior, I guess."

Somehow, I doubted that.

Michael seemed to sense that I wasn't buying it. "And also possibly because Briggs needed someone to read your emotions and figure out whether or not you're a secret bottle of rage who shouldn't be granted access to confidential files."

"Did I pass?" I asked, a teasing note making its way into my voice.

"Uh-uh-uh," Michael replied. "That's four questions."

With no warning, he jerked the steering wheel to the left, pulled a U-turn, and then took a fast right. A few seconds later, the two of us slammed into a parking space at what appeared to be some kind of airport hangar.

"What," I said, my eyes widening as I took in the sleek hunk of metal in front of us, "is that?"

"That?" Michael repeated. "That's the jet."

"Let me guess," I said, only half joking. "You made getting to keep your private jet a condition of your acceptance into the program?"

Michael snorted. "Sadly, it belongs to the FBI. When Briggs isn't out roping the young and impressionable into doing his dirty work for him, he belongs to a specialized team that works with law enforcement across the country. The jet cuts down on travel time. For us, it's just a perk."

"Cassie," Agent Briggs greeted me the second I stepped out of the car. Just my name, nothing else.

Michael hit a button, and the trunk popped open. I went to retrieve my bag, and Michael shot Briggs a very good imitation of Nonna's scowl. "You just going to stand there?" he asked the FBI agent.

Briggs helped me with my bag, and Michael caught my eye. "Amused," he whispered. "And also some residual embarrassment."

It took me a second to realize that Michael wasn't interpreting Briggs's facial expression. He was interpreting mine.

I'll stop trying to read your emotions if you stop trying to profile me.

Liar.

Without another word, Michael turned and sauntered to the jet. By the time I climbed aboard, he was already lounging in the back row of seats. He looked up, his posture inviting, his eyes telling me to stay away.

Tearing my gaze from his, I took a seat in the row in front of him, facing the cockpit. We'd see how good he was at reading my emotions based on nothing more than the back of my head.

"Tell you what," Michael whispered, his voice loud enough to reach my ears, but not Briggs's. "If you promise not to give me the silent treatment, I'll give you a fourth question, free of charge."

As the plane took off and the city grew small behind us, I turned around in my chair.

"You're leaving the Porsche in Denver?" I asked.

He leaned forward, close enough that his forehead was almost touching mine.

"The devil's in the details, Cassie. I never said that Porsche was my only car."

YOU

It's been days since the last time, days of reliving your failure, over and over again. Each minute has been torture, and now you're on a schedule. You don't have the luxury of hunting for the perfect girl. The right girl. There's nothing special about the one you've chosen, except for the color of her hair.

It reminds you of someone else's hair, and that's enough. For now.

You kill her in a motel room. No one sees you enter. No one will see you leave. You put duct tape over her mouth. You have to imagine the sound of her screams, but the look in her eyes is worth it.

It's fast, but not too fast.

It's yours.

You're in charge. You decide. You slide the knife into the flesh under her cheekbone. You carve the heavy makeup— and the skin—off of her face.

There. That's better.

You feel better. More in control. And you know that even though you don't have time for pictures, you'll never forget the way the blood looks as it stains her hair.

Some days, you think, it feels like you have been doing this forever. But no matter how many there are, no matter how proficient you've become at showing them what you are, what they are, there is a part of you that knows.

It will never be quite right.

It will never be perfect.

There will never be another one like the first.

PART TWO:
LEARNING

CHAPTER 7

I stepped off the jet and blinked, my eyes adjusting to the sun. A woman with bright red hair strode toward the plane. She was wearing a gray suit and black sunglasses, and she walked like she had someplace to be.

"I heard a rumor we were getting in around the same time," she called out to Briggs. "Thought I'd come to greet you in person." Without waiting for a reply, she turned her attention to me. "I'm Special Agent Lacey Locke. Briggs is my partner, and you're Cassandra Hobbes."

She timed this speech to end just as she closed the space between us. She held out a hand, and I was struck by the fact that she looked somehow impish despite the sunglasses and the suit.

I took her hand. "It's nice to meet you," I said. "Most people just call me Cassie."

"Cassie it is, then," she replied. "Briggs tells me you're one of mine."

One of hers?

Michael filled in the blank. "A profiler."

"Don't sound so enthusiastic about the science of profiling, Michael," Locke said lightly. "Cassie might mistake you for a seventeen-year-old boy *without* a strong sense of derision for the rest of the world."

Michael held a hand to his chest. "Your sarcasm wounds me, Agent Locke."

She snorted.

"You're home early," Briggs cut in, aiming the comment at Agent Locke. "Nothing in Boise?"

Locke gave a brief jerk of her head. "Dead end."

An unspoken communication passed between the two of them, and then Briggs turned to me. "As Michael so obligingly pointed out, Agent Locke is a profiler. She'll be in charge of your training."

"Lucky you," Locke said with a grin.

"Are you . . ." I wasn't sure how to ask.

"A Natural?" she said. "No. There's only one thing I've ever been a natural at, and sadly, I can't tell you about that until you're twenty-one. But I did go through the FBI Academy and took every class they offered in behavioral analysis. I've been a part of the behavioral science unit for almost three years."

I wondered if it would be rude to ask how old she was now.

"Twenty-nine," she said. "And don't worry, you'll get used to it."

"Used to what?"

She grinned again. "People answering questions before you ask them."

The program's base of operations was a looming Victorian-style house in the tiny town of Quantico, Virginia—close enough to FBI headquarters on Marine Corps Base Quantico to be handy, but not so close that people were going to start asking questions.

"Living room. Media room. Library. Study." The person that Briggs had found to look after the house—and us—was a retired marine by the name of Judd Hawkins. He was sixty-something, eagle-eyed, and a man of few words. "Kitchen's through there. Your room is on the second floor." Judd paused for a fraction of a second to look at me. "You'll be sharing with one of the other girls. I expect that's not a problem?"

I shook my head, and he strode back down the hallway and toward a staircase. "Look alive, Ms. Hobbes," he called back. I hurried to catch up and thought I heard a smile in his voice, though there was barely a hint of it on his face.

I fought a smile of my own. Judd Hawkins might have

been gruff and no-nonsense, but my gut was telling me he had more soft spots than most people would have thought.

He caught me studying him and gave a brisk, business-like nod. Like Briggs, he didn't seem to mind the idea that I might be getting a general picture of his personality from the little details.

Unlike a certain other individual I could think of, who'd done his best to thwart me at every turn.

Refusing to glance back at Michael, I noticed a series of framed pictures lining the staircase. A dozen or so men. One woman. Most were in their late twenties or early thirties, but one or two were older. Some were smiling; some were not. A paunchy man with dark eyebrows and thinning hair hung between a handsome heartbreaker and a black-and-white photo from the turn of the century. At the top of the stairs, an elderly couple smiled out from a slightly larger portrait.

I glanced at Judd, wondering if these were his relatives, or if they belonged to someone else in this house.

"They're killers." An Asian girl about my age stepped around the corner. She moved like a cat—and smiled like she'd just eaten a canary.

"The people in the pictures," she clarified. "They're serial killers." She twirled her shiny black ponytail around her index finger, clearly enjoying my discomfort. "It's the program's cheery way of reminding Dean why he's here."

Dean? Who was Dean?

"Personally, I think it's a little macabre, but then again, I'm not a profiler." The girl flicked her ponytail. "You are, though. Aren't you?"

She took a step forward, and my eyes were drawn to her footwear: black leather boots with heels high enough to make my feet shudder in spasms of sympathy. She was wearing skintight black pants and a high-necked sleeveless sweater, electric blue to match the streaks in her black hair.

As I took in her clothing, the girl closed the space between us until she was standing so close to me that I thought she might reach out and start twirling my hair instead of her own.

"Lia," Judd said, absolutely unfazed, "this is Cassie. If you're finished trying to scare her, I'm betting she'd really like to set that bag down."

Lia shrugged. *"Mi casa es su casa.* Your room is through there."

"Your" room, I thought. *Not "our" room.*

"Cassie's really broken up about not rooming with you, Lia," Michael said, interpreting my facial expression with a wink. Lia pivoted to face him, and her lips twisted upward in a slow, sizzling grin.

"Miss me?" she asked.

"Like a thorn in my paw," Michael replied.

Coming up the stairs behind us, Agent Briggs cleared his throat. "Lia," he said. "Nice to see you."

Lia gave him a look. "Now, Agent Briggs," she replied, "that's simply not true."

Agent Locke rolled her eyes. "Lia's specialty is deception," she told me. "She has an uncanny knack for being able to tell when people are lying. And," Agent Locke added, meeting Lia's eyes, "she's a very good liar."

Lia didn't seem to take offense at the agent's words. "I'm also bilingual," she said. "And very, very flexible."

The second *very* was aimed directly at Michael.

"So," I said, my duffel bag digging into my shoulder as I tried to process the fact that Lia was a Natural liar, "the pictures on the wall *aren't* serial killers?"

That question was answered with silence. Silence from Michael. Silence from Judd. Silence from Agent Locke, who looked a bit abashed.

Agent Briggs cleared his throat. "No," he said finally. "That's true."

My eyes were drawn to the portrait of the elderly couple.

Smiling serial killers, five-inch heels, and a girl with a gift for lying? This was going to be interesting.

CHAPTER 8

Briggs and Locke left shortly after Judd showed me to my room. They promised to return the next day for training, but for now, all that was expected of me was to settle in. My roommate—whoever she was—had yet to make an appearance, so for the moment, I had the room to myself.

Twin beds sat at opposite ends of the room. A bay window overlooked the backyard. Tentatively, I opened what I assumed to be the closet door. The closet was exactly half full: half of each rack, half of the floor space, half of the shelves. My roommate favored patterns to solids, bright colors to pastels, and had a healthy amount of black and white in her wardrobe, but no gray.

All of her shoes were flats.

"Dial it back a notch, Cassie," I told myself. I'd have months to analyze my roommate's personality—*without* creepily stalking her half of the closet. Quickly and efficiently, I emptied my own bag. I'd lived in Colorado for five years, but before that, the longest I'd ever lived in one place was four months. My mother was always off to the next show, the next town, the next mark, and I was an expert unpacker.

There was still space on my side of the closet when I was done.

"Knock-knock." Lia's voice was high and clear. She didn't wait for permission before coming into the room, and I realized with a start that she'd changed clothes.

The boots had been replaced with ballet flats, and she'd traded the tight black pants for a lacy, flowing skirt. Her hair was pulled back at the nape of her neck, and even her eyes looked softer.

It was like she'd given herself a makeover—or switched personalities altogether.

First Michael, now Lia. I wondered if he'd picked up the trick of changing clothing styles from her, or if she'd gotten it from him. Given that Lia was the one who specialized in deception, my money was on the former.

"Are you finished unpacking yet?" she asked.

"I'm still working on some stuff," I said, busying myself with the dresser.

"No. You're not."

I'd never considered myself a liar until that moment, when Lia's ability took the option away.

"Look, those serial killer pictures give new meaning to the word *creepy*." Lia leaned back against the doorjamb. "I was here for six weeks before someone told me that Grandma and Gramps were actually Faye and Ray Copeland, who were convicted of killing five people and made a cozy little quilt out of their clothes. Trust me, it's better that you know now."

"Thanks," I said dryly.

"Anyway," Lia said, dragging out the word, "Judd gives crappy tours. He's a surprisingly decent cook, and he's got eyes in the back of his head, but he's not exactly what one would call *chatty*, and unless we're about to burn the place down, he's pretty hands-off. I thought you might want a real tour. Or that you might have some questions."

I wasn't sure that a person renowned for her skill at lying was the ideal information source *or* tour guide, but I wasn't about to turn down a peace offering, and I did have one question.

"Where's my roommate?"

"Where she always is," Lia replied innocently. "The basement."

The basement ran the length of the house and stretched out underneath the front and back yards. From the bottom of the stairs, all I could see was two enormous white walls that ran the width of the space, but didn't quite reach the fourteen-foot ceilings. There was a small space between where one wall ended and the next began.

An entrance.

I walked toward it. Something exploded, and I jumped backward, my hands flying up in front of my face.

Glass, I thought belatedly. *Shattering glass.*

A second later, I realized that I couldn't see the source of the sound. I lowered my hands and looked back at Lia, who hadn't so much as flinched.

"Is that normal?" I asked her.

She gave a graceful little shrug. "Define *normal.*"

A girl poked her head out from behind one of the partitions. "Conforming to a type, standard, or regular pattern."

The first thing I noticed about the girl—other than the chipper tone in her voice and the fact that she had literally just defined *normal*—was her hair. It was blond, glow-in-the-dark pale, and stick straight. The ends were uneven and her blunt-cut bangs were too short, like she'd chopped them off herself.

"Aren't you supposed to be wearing safety goggles?" Lia asked.

"It is possible that my goggles have been compromised." With that, the girl disappeared back behind the partition.

Based on the self-satisfied curve of Lia's lips, I was going to go out on a limb and guess that I had just met my roommate.

"Sloane, Cassie," Lia said with a grand gesture. "Cassie, Sloane."

"Nice to meet you," I said. I took a few steps forward, until I was standing in the space between the partitions and could see what they had hidden before. A narrow hallway stretched out in front of me. It was lined with rooms on either side. Each room had only three walls.

Immediately to my left, I found Sloane standing in the middle of what appeared to be a bathroom. There was a door on the far side, and I realized that the space looked exactly the way a bathroom would if someone had removed the back wall.

"Like a movie set," I murmured. There was glass all over the floor, and at least a hundred Post-it notes stuck to the edge of the sink and scattered in a spiral pattern on the tiles. I glanced back down the hallway at the other rooms. The other sets.

"Potential crime scene," Lia corrected. "For simulations. On this side"—Lia posed like a game show assistant—"we have interior locations: bathrooms, bedrooms, kitchens, foyers. A couple of miniature—and I do mean *miniature*— restaurant sets, and, just because we really are that cliché, a mock post office, for all your *going postal* needs."

Lia pivoted and gestured toward the other side of the hall. "And over here," she said, "we have a few outdoor scenes: park, parking lot, make-out point."

I turned back to the bathroom set and Sloane. She knelt gingerly next to the shards of glass on the floor and stared at them. Her face was calm. Her fingers hovered just over the carnage.

After a long moment, she blinked and stood up. "Your hair is red."

"Yes," I said. "It is."

"People with red hair require roughly twenty percent more anesthesia to undergo surgery, and they're significantly more likely to wake up on the table."

I got the distinct feeling that this was Sloane's version of "hello," and suddenly, everything clicked into place: the prevalence of patterns in her wardrobe, the precision with which she'd divided our closet in two. "Agent Briggs said that someone here was a Natural with numbers and probabilities."

"Sloane's absolutely dangerous with anything numerical," Lia said. She gestured lazily toward the glass shards. "Sometimes literally."

"It was just a test," Sloane said defensively. "The algorithm that predicts the scatter pattern of the shards is really quite—"

"Fascinating?" a voice behind us suggested. Lia dragged one long, manicured nail over her bottom lip. I turned around.

Michael smiled. "You should see her when she's had caffeine," he told me, nodding at Sloane.

"Michael," Sloane said darkly, "hides the coffee."

"Trust me," Michael drawled, "it's a kindness to us all." He paused and then gave me a long, slow smile. "These two have you nice and traumatized yet, Colorado?"

I processed the fact that he'd just given me a nickname, and Lia stepped in between us. "Traumatized?" she repeated. "It's almost like you don't trust me, Michael." Her eyes widened and her lower lip poked out.

Michael snorted. "Wonder why."

An emotion reader, a deception specialist, a statistician who could not be allowed to ingest coffee, and me.

"Is this it?" I asked. "Just the four of us?"

Hadn't Lia mentioned someone else?

Michael's eyes darkened. Lia's mouth curved slowly into a smile.

"Well," Sloane said brightly, completely unaware of the changing undercurrent in the room. "There's also Dean."

CHAPTER 9

e found Dean in the garage. He was lying on a black bench, facing away from the door. Dark blond hair was plastered to his face with sweat, his jaw clenched as he executed a series of slow and methodical bench presses. Each time his elbows locked, I wondered if he'd stop. Each time, he kept going.

He was muscular but lean, and my first impression was that this wasn't a workout. This was punishment.

Michael rolled his eyes and then strolled up behind Dean. "Ninety-eight," he said, his tone full of mock pain. "Ninety-nine. One hundred!"

Dean closed his eyes for a brief moment, then pushed the barbell up again. His arms shook slightly as he went to set the weight down. Michael clearly had no intention of spotting him. To my surprise, Sloane pushed past Michael, wrapped dainty little hands around the barbell, and rocked back on her heels, angling it into place.

Dean wiped his hands on his jeans, grabbed a nearby towel, and sat up. "Thanks," he told Sloane.

"Torque," she said, instead of *you're welcome*. "The role of the lever was played by my arms."

Dean stood up, his lips angling slightly upward, but the moment he saw me, the fledgling smile froze on his face.

"Dean Redding," Michael said, enjoying Dean's sudden obvious discomfort a little too much, "meet Cassie Hobbes."

"Nice to meet you," Dean said, pulling dark eyes from mine and directing those words at the floor.

Lia, who'd been remarkably quiet up to this point, raised an eyebrow at Dean. "Well," she said, "that's not strictly—"

"Lia." Dean's voice wasn't loud or hard, but the second he said her name, Lia stopped.

"That's not strictly what?" I asked, even though I knew that the next word out of her mouth would have been *true*.

"Never mind," Lia said in a singsong tone.

I looked back at Dean: *Light hair. Dark eyes. Open posture. Clenched fists.*

I cataloged the way he was standing, the lines of his face, the dingy white T-shirt and ratty blue jeans. His hair needed to be cut, and he stood with his back to the wall, his face cast in shadows, like that was where he belonged.

Why wasn't it nice to meet me?

"Dean," Michael said, with the air of someone imparting a fascinating bit of useless trivia, "is a Natural profiler. Just like you."

Those last three words seemed more aimed at Dean than me, and as they hit their target, Dean lifted his eyes to meet Michael's. There was no emotion on Dean's face, but there was *something* in his eyes, and I found myself expecting Michael to look away first.

"Dean," Michael continued, staring at Dean and talking to me, "knows more about the way that killers think than just about anyone."

Dean threw down the towel in his hand. Muscles taut, he brushed by Michael and Sloane, by Lia, by me. A few seconds later, he was gone.

"Dean has a temper," Michael told me, leaning back against the workout bench.

Lia snorted. "Michael, if Dean had a temper, you'd be dead."

"Dean's not going to kill anyone," Sloane said, her voice almost comically serious.

Michael dug a quarter out of his pocket and flipped it in the air. "Wanna bet?"

— — —

That night, I didn't dream. I also didn't sleep much, courtesy of the fact that Sloane, who had a dainty little build, also apparently had the nasal passages of an overweight trucker. Instead, as I tried to block out the sound of her snoring, I closed my eyes and pictured each of the Naturals who lived in this house. *Michael. Dean. Lia. Sloane.* None of them was what I'd expected. None of them fit a familiar mold. As I drifted into that half-awake, half-asleep state that was as close as I was going to get to a real night's rest, I played a game I'd invented when I was little. I mentally peeled off my own skin and put on someone else's.

Lia's.

I started with the physical things. She was taller than I was, and lithe. Her hair was longer, and instead of sleeping with it tucked under her head, she would spread it out on the pillow. Her fingernails were painted, and when she had energy to burn, she rubbed the thumbnail on her left hand with the thumb on her right. In my mind, I turned my head—Lia's head—to the side, peering into her closet.

If Michael had leveraged a car out of Briggs, Lia would have gone for clothes. I could almost *see* the closet, full to overflowing. As the room came more into focus, I could feel my subconscious taking over, feel myself losing the real world in favor of this imaginary one I'd built in my head.

I let go of my bed and my closet, my physical sensations.

I let myself *be* Lia, and a rush of information came at me from all sides. Like a writer getting lost in a book, I let the simulation run its course. Where Sloane and I were neat, the Lia in my head was messy, her room a multisensory archive of the past few months. There was no rhyme or reason to the organization of the closet. Dresses hung half on and half off the hangers. There were clothes—dirty, clean, new, and everything in between—on the floor.

I pictured getting out of bed. In my own body, I had a tendency to sit up first, but Lia wouldn't take the time. She'd roll out of bed, ready for action. Ready to attack. Long hair fell on my shoulders, and I twirled a strand of it around my index finger: another of Lia's nervous habits, designed to look like it wasn't nervous at all.

I glanced over at the door to the room. Closed, of course. Probably also locked. Who was I keeping out? What was I afraid of?

Afraid? I scoffed silently, my mind-voice sounding more and more like Lia's. *I'm not* afraid *of anything.*

I walked over to the closet—light on my toes, hips swaying gently—and pulled out the first shirt I touched. The selection was completely random, but what came next wasn't. I built the outfit up around me. I dressed myself up like a doll, and with each passing moment, I put that much more space between the surface and everything underneath.

I did my hair, my eyes, my nails.

But there was still that little voice in my head. The same one that had insisted I wasn't scared. Only this time, the one thing it kept saying, over and over again, was that I was here—behind this locked door with who knows what waiting outside—because I had nowhere else to go.

YOU

You're home now. You're alone. Everything is in its place. Everything but this.

You know that there are other people like you. Other monsters. Other gods. You know you're not the only one who takes keepsakes, things to remember the girls by, once their screams and their bodies and their begging-pleading-lying lips are gone.

You walk slowly to the cabinet. You open it. Carefully, gingerly, you place this whore's lipstick next to all the rest. The authorities won't notice it's missing when they search her purse.

They never do.

A lazy smile on your face, you run your fingertips across each one. Remembering. Savoring. Planning.

Because it's never enough. It's never over.

Especially now.

CHAPTER 10

he next day, I could barely look at Lia. The game I'd played the night before was one my younger self had played with strangers: children I'd met in diners, people who had come to my mother's shows. They were never real to me—and neither were the things I'd imagined once I'd mentally tried on their shoes. But now I had to wonder how much of it was really imagination and how much of it was my subconscious working its way through Lia's BPE.

Had I imagined that Lia was messy—or had I profiled it?

"There's cereal in the cabinet and eggs in the fridge," Judd greeted me from behind a newspaper as I wandered into the kitchen, still debating that question. "I'm making a grocery run at oh-nine-hundred. If you've got requests, speak now or forever hold your peace."

"No requests," I said.

"Low maintenance," Judd commented.

I shrugged. "I try."

Judd folded his paper, carried an empty mug to the sink, and rinsed it out. A minute later—at nine o'clock on the dot—I was alone in the kitchen. As I poured myself a bowl of cereal, I went back to trying to work my way through the logic of my Lia simulation, to figure out how I knew what I knew—and if I knew it at all.

"I have no idea what those Cheerios did to you, but I'm sure they're very, very sorry," Michael said as he slid into the seat next to me at the kitchen table.

"Excuse me?"

"You've been stirring them into submission for a good five minutes," Michael told me. "It's spoon violence, is what it is."

I picked up a Cheerio and flicked it at him. Michael caught it and popped it into his mouth.

"So which one of us was it this time?" Michael asked.

Suddenly, I became very interested in my Cheerios.

"Come on, Colorado. When your brain starts profiling, your face starts broadcasting a mix of concentration, curiosity, and calm." Michael paused. I took a big bite of cereal. "The muscles in your neck relax," he continued. "Your lips turn ever so subtly down. Your head tilts slightly to one side, and you get crow's-feet at the corners of your eyes."

I set my spoon calmly in my bowl. "I do not get crow's-feet."

Michael helped himself to my spoon—and a bite of cereal. "Anyone ever tell you you're cute when you're annoyed?"

"I hope I'm not interrupting." Lia came in, stole the cereal box, and started eating right out of the carton. "Actually, that's not true. Whatever's going on here, I am absolutely delighted to interrupt it."

I tried to keep myself from studying Lia—and I definitely tried to keep from wrinkling the corners of my eyes—but it was hard to ignore the fact that she was wearing barely-there silk pajamas. And pearls.

"So, Cassie, are you ready for your first day of How to Crawl into the Skulls of Bad Guys 101?" Lia set the cereal box down and headed for the fridge. Her head disappeared into the refrigerator as she started digging around. Her pajama bottoms left very little to the imagination.

"I'm ready," I said, averting my eyes.

"Cassie was born ready," Michael declared. Over in the refrigerator, Lia stopped rummaging for a moment. "Besides," Michael continued, "whatever Agent Locke has her doing, it has to be better than watching foreign-language films. Without the subtitles."

I bit back a smile at the aggrieved tone in Michael's voice. "Is that what they had you do on your first day?"

"That," Michael said, "is what they had me do for my first *month*. 'Emotions aren't about what people say,'" he mimicked, "'they're about posture, facial expressions, and culture-specific instantiations of universal phenomenological experiences.'"

Lia exited the refrigerator with empty hands, shut the door, and opened the freezer. "Poor baby," she told Michael. "I've been here for almost three years, and the only thing they've taught me is that psychopaths are really good liars, and FBI agents are really bad ones."

"Have you met many?" I asked.

"FBI agents?" Lia feigned ignorance as she retrieved a carton of mint-chocolate-chip ice cream from the freezer.

I gave her a look. "Psychopaths."

She grabbed a spoon out of the drawer and brandished it like a magic wand. "The FBI hides us away in a nice little house in a nice little neighborhood in a nice little town. Do you really think Briggs is going to let me tag along on prison interviews? Or go into the field, where I might actually get to *do* something?"

Michael put Lia's words in slightly more diplomatic terms. "The Bureau has tapes," he said. "And reels and transcripts. Cold cases, mostly. Things that other people haven't ever been able to solve. And for every cold case they bring us, there are dozens of cases that they've already solved. Tests to see if we really are as good as Agent Briggs says we are."

"Even when you give them the answer they're looking for," Lia continued, picking up right where Michael left off, "even when the Powers That Be know that you're right, they want to know why."

Why what? This time, I didn't ask the question out loud—but Michael answered it anyway.

"Why we can do it and they can't." He reached over and snagged another bite of my Cheerios. "They don't just want to train us. They don't just want to use us. They want to *be* us."

"Absolutely," a new voice concurred. "Deep down, in my heart of hearts, all I really want is to be Michael Townsend."

Agent Locke strolled into the kitchen and went straight for the fridge. Clearly she was at home here, even if she lived somewhere else.

"Briggs left files for you two"—Agent Locke gestured to Michael and Lia—"in his study. He's going to run a new simulation with Sloane today, and *I'm* going to start catching Cassie up to speed." She heaved a larger-than-life sigh. "It's not as glamorous as being a jaded seventeen-year-old boy with parental issues and a hair-gel dependency, but *c'est la vie.*"

Michael reached up to scratch the side of his face—and oh-so-subtly flipped Agent Locke off in the process.

Lia twirled her spoon around her finger, a tiny, ice-cream-laden baton. "Lacey Locke, everybody," she said, like the FBI agent was a comedian and Lia the announcer.

Locke grinned. "Doesn't Judd have a rule about you

wearing lingerie in the kitchen?" she asked, eyeing Lia's pajamas. Lia shrugged, but something about Agent Locke's presence seemed to subdue her. Within minutes, my fellow Naturals had scattered. Neither Lia nor Michael seemed anxious to spend time in the company of an FBI profiler.

"I hope they're not making life too difficult on you," Locke said.

"No." In fact, for a moment there, eating with the two of them, talking to them, had felt natural.

No pun intended.

"Neither Michael nor Lia was given much of a choice about joining the program." Locke waited for that to sink in. "That tends to put a chip on a person's shoulder."

"They're not the type to respond well to being strong-armed," I said slowly.

"No," Agent Locke replied. "They aren't. I've made a lot of mistakes, but that wasn't one of mine. Briggs lacks a certain amount of . . . *finesse*. Guy never met a square peg he didn't want to pound into a round hole."

That description fit with my impression of Agent Briggs exactly. Agent Locke was speaking my language, but I didn't have time to relish that fact.

Because Dean was standing in the doorway.

Agent Locke saw him and nodded. "Right on time."

"On time for what?" I asked.

Dean answered on Agent Locke's behalf, but unlike

the red-haired agent, he wasn't smiling. He wasn't friendly. He didn't want to be there—and unless I was mistaken, he didn't like me.

"For your first lesson."

CHAPTER 11

f Dean was unhappy at the prospect of spending the morning with me, he was even less pleased when Agent Locke's plan for my first day required us to take a little field trip. Clearly, he'd expected a pen-and-paper lesson, or possibly a simulation in the basement, but Agent Locke just tossed him the keys to her SUV.

"You're driving."

Most FBI agents wouldn't have insisted a seventeen-year-old boy drive—but it was becoming increasingly clear to me that Lacey Locke wasn't most agents. She took the front passenger seat, and I slid into the back.

"Where to?" Dean asked Agent Locke as he backed out of the driveway. She gave him an address, and he murmured a reply. I tried to diagnose the slight twinge of an accent I heard in his voice.

Southern.

He didn't say a single word for the rest of the drive. I tried to get a read on him. He didn't seem shy. Maybe he was the type of person who saved his words for those rare occasions when he really had something to say. Maybe he kept to himself and used silence as a way of keeping other people at arm's length.

Or maybe he just had zero desire to converse with Locke and me.

He's a Natural profiler, I thought, wondering if his brain was churning, too, assimilating details about me the way I was assessing him.

He was a careful driver.

His shoulders tensed when someone cut him off.

And when we arrived at our destination, he got out of the car, shut the door, and held the keys out to Agent Locke— all without ever looking at me. I was used to fading into the background, but somehow, coming from Dean, it felt like an insult. Like I wasn't worth profiling, like he didn't have the slightest interest in figuring me out.

"Welcome to Westside Mall," Agent Locke said, snapping me out of it. "I'm sure this isn't what you were expecting for your first day, Cassie, but I wanted to get a sense of what you can do with normal people before we dive into the abnormal end of the spectrum."

Dean flicked his eyes sideways.

Locke called him on it. "Something you'd like to add?"

Dean stuffed his hands into his pockets. "It's just been a long time," he said, "since someone asked me to think about *normal.*"

Five minutes later, we had a table in the food court.

"The woman in the purple fleece," Agent Locke said. "What can you tell me about her, Cassie?"

I sat and followed her gaze to the woman in question. Midtwenties. She was wearing running shoes and jeans in addition to the fleece. Either she was sporty and she'd thrown on the jeans because she was coming to the mall, or she wasn't, but wanted people to think that she was. I said as much out loud.

"What *else* can you tell me?" Agent Locke asked.

My gut told me that Agent Locke didn't want details. She wanted the big picture.

Behavior. Personality. Environment.

I tried to integrate Purple Fleece into her surroundings. She'd chosen a seat near the edge of the food court, even though there were plenty of tables available closer to the restaurant where she'd purchased her meal. There were several people sitting near her, but she stayed focused on her food.

"She's a student," I said finally. "Graduate school of some kind—my money's on med school. She's not married, but has a serious boyfriend. She comes from an upper-middle-class family, heavy emphasis on the *upper.* She's a runner, but not a health nut. She most likely gets up early, likes doing things that other people find painful, and if she has any siblings, they're either younger than she is or they're all boys."

I waited for Agent Locke to reply. She didn't. Neither did Dean.

To fill the silence, I added one last observation. "She gets cold really easily."

There was no other excuse for wearing a fleece—even indoors—in July.

"What makes you think she's a student?" Agent Locke asked finally.

I met Dean's eyes and knew suddenly that he saw it, too. "It's ten thirty in the morning," I said, "and she's not at work. It's too early for a lunch break, and she's not dressed like someone who's on the job."

Agent Locke raised an eyebrow. "Maybe she works from home. Or maybe she's between jobs. Maybe she teaches elementary school and she's on summer vacation."

Those objections were perfectly valid, but somehow—to me—they still felt wrong. It was hard to explain; I thought of Michael warning me that the FBI would never stop trying to figure out how I did what I did.

I thought about Agent Locke saying she'd learned profiling the hard way—one class at a time.

"She's not even looking at them."

To my shock, Dean was the one who came to my rescue.

"Pardon?" Agent Locke turned her attention to him.

"The other people here in her age range." Dean nodded toward a couple of young moms with small children, plus several department store employees lined up for coffee. "She's not looking at them. They aren't her peers. She doesn't even realize they're the same age. She pays more attention to college students than to other adults, but she clearly doesn't consider herself one of them, either."

And that was the feeling I hadn't been able to put into words. It was like Dean could see into my head, make sense of the information bouncing around my brain—but, of course, that wasn't it. He hadn't needed to get into my head, because he'd been thinking the exact same thing.

After a long moment of silence, Dean flicked his eyes over to me. "Why med school?"

I glanced back at the girl. "Because she's a runner."

Dean smiled, ever so slightly. "You mean she's a masochist."

Across the room, the girl we'd been talking about rose, and I was able to make out the bags in her hand, the stores she'd shopped at. It fit. Everything fit.

I wasn't wrong.

"What makes you think she has a boyfriend?" Dean asked, and under his quiet drawl I could hear curiosity— and maybe even admiration.

I shrugged in response to his question—mainly because

I didn't want to tell him that the reason I'd been sure this girl wasn't single was the fact that the entire time we'd been there, she hadn't so much as glanced at Dean.

From a distance, he would have looked older.

Even in jeans and a faded black T-shirt, you could see the muscles tensing against the fabric of his sleeves. And the muscles not covered by his sleeves.

His hair, his eyes, the way he stood, and the way he moved—if she'd been single, she would have looked.

"New game," Agent Locke said. "I point to the car, you tell me about the person who owns it."

We'd been at the mall for three hours. I'd thought coming out to the parking lot had signaled the end of today's training, but apparently I was wrong.

"That one, Cassie. Go."

I opened my mouth, then shut it again. I was used to starting with people: their posture, the way they talked, their clothes, their occupations, their gender, the way they arranged a napkin on their lap—that was my language. Starting with a car was like flying blind.

"In our line of work," Agent Locke told me as I stared at a white Acura, debating whether it belonged to a shopper or someone who worked at the mall, "you don't get to meet the suspect before you profile the crime. You go to the scene and you rebuild what happened. You take physical evidence, you turn it into behavior, and then you try to narrow down the range of suspects. You don't know if you're looking for a man or a woman, a teenager or an old man. You know how they killed, but you don't know why. You know how they left the body, but you have to figure out how they found the victim." She paused. "So, Cassie. Who owns this car?"

The make and model weren't telling me much. This car could have belonged to either a man or a woman, and it was parked in front of the food court, which meant that I had no idea what the owner's destination inside the mall was. The parking space wasn't a good one, but it wasn't bad. The parking job left a little to be desired.

"They were in a hurry," I said. "The parking job is crooked, and they didn't bother cruising for a better space." That also told me that the driver didn't have the kind of ego that would push a person to hunt for a prime spot, as if getting a great parking place at the mall was an indicator of personal worth. "No car seat, so no young children. No bumper stickers, relatively recently washed. They're not here for food—no reason to hurry for that—but they parked at the food court, so either they don't know where they're going once they get inside the mall or their store of choice is close by."

I paused, waiting for Dean to pick up where I had left off, but he didn't. Instead, Agent Locke gave me a single piece of advice.

"Don't say *they*."

"I didn't mean *they* as in plural," I said hastily. "I just haven't decided yet if it's a man or a woman."

Dean glanced at the mall entrance and then back at me. "That's not what she means. *They* keeps you on the outside. So do *he* and *she*."

"So what word am I supposed to use?"

"Officially," Agent Locke said, "we use the term *Unknown Subject*—or *UNSUB*."

"And unofficially?" I asked.

Dean shoved his hands into the pockets of his jeans. "If you want to climb inside someone's head," he said roughly, "you use the word *I*."

The night before, I'd imagined myself in Lia's body, imagined what it was like to be her. I could imagine driving this car, parking it like this, climbing out—but this wasn't about cars. Ultimately, I wouldn't be profiling shoppers.

I'd be profiling killers.

"What if I don't want to be them?" I asked. I knew that if I closed my eyes, if I so much as blinked, I would be right back in my mother's dressing room. I'd be able to see the blood. I'd be able to smell it. "What if I can't?"

"Then you're lucky." Dean's voice was quiet, but his eyes were hard. "And you'd be better off at home."

My stomach twisted. He didn't think I belonged here.

Suddenly, it was all too easy to remember that when we'd met the day before and he'd said "nice to meet you," it had been a lie.

Agent Locke set a hand on my shoulder. "If you want to get close to an UNSUB, but you don't want to put yourself in their shoes, there's another word you can use."

I turned my back on Dean and focused my full attention on Agent Locke. "And what word is that?" I asked.

Locke met my gaze. "*You.*"

CHAPTER 12

That night, I dreamed that I was walking through a
narrow hallway. The floor was tiled. The walls were
white. The only sound in the entire room was my
sneaker-clad feet scuffing against the freshly mopped floor.

This isn't right. Something about this isn't right.

Fluorescent lights flickered overhead, and on the ground,
my shadow flickered, too. At the end of the hallway, there
was a metal door, painted to match the walls. It was slightly
ajar, and I wondered if I'd left it that way or if my mother
had cracked the door open to keep an eye out for me.

Don't go in there. Stop. You have to stop.

I smiled and kept right on walking. One step, two steps,
three steps, four. On some level, I knew that this was a
dream, knew what I would find when I opened that door—
but I couldn't stop. My body felt numb from the waist down.
My smile hurt.

I laid my hand flat against the metal door and pushed.

"Cassie?"

My mother was standing there, dressed in blue. A breath caught in my throat—not because she was beautiful, though she was, and not because she was on the verge of scolding me for taking so long to report back on the crowd.

A vise closed in around my lungs, because this was wrong. This hadn't happened, and I wished to God it had.

Please don't be a dream. Just this once, let it be real. Don't let it—

"Cassie?" My mom stumbled backward. She fell. Blood turned blue silk red. It splattered against the walls. There was so much of it—too much.

She's crawling in it, slipping, but everywhere she goes, the knife is there.

Hands grabbed at her ankles. I turned, trying to see her attacker's face, and just like that, my mother was gone and I was back outside the door. My hand pushed it open.

This is how it happened, I thought dully. *This is real.*

I stepped into the darkness. I felt something wet and squishy beneath my feet, and the smell—oh, God, the smell. I scrambled for the light switch.

Don't. Don't turn it on, don't—

I woke with a start.

In the bed beside me, Sloane was dead to the world. I'd had the dream often enough to know that there was no point in closing my eyes again. I crept quietly out of bed and went to the window. I needed to do something—to take my cue from the woman I'd profiled that morning and run until my body hurt, or to follow in Dean's footsteps and take it out on some weights. Then I caught sight of the backyard—and more specifically, the pool.

The yard was dimly lit, the water gleaming black in the moonlight. Silently, I grabbed a swimsuit and slipped out of the room without waking Sloane. Minutes later, I was sitting at the edge of the pool. Even in the dead of night, the air was hot. I dangled my legs over the edge.

I lowered myself into the pool. Slowly, the tension left my body. My brain shut off. For a few minutes, I just treaded water, listening to the sounds of the neighborhood at nighttime: crickets and the wind and my hands moving through the water. Then I stopped—stopped treading water, stopped fighting the pull of gravity—and let myself sink.

I opened my eyes underwater, but couldn't see anything. There was darkness all around me, and then suddenly, there was a flicker of light at the pool's surface.

I wasn't alone.

You don't know that, I told myself, but I saw the faintest blur of motion, and that protest died a quick and brutal death. There was someone up there—and I couldn't stay underwater indefinitely.

Just like that, I felt like I was back in the narrow hallway of my dreams, walking slowly toward something awful.

It's nothing.

Still, I fought the need for air. I wanted—irrationally—to stay underwater, where it was safe. But I couldn't. Water plugged my ears, and as my lungs screamed for air, the sound of my own heartbeat surrounded me.

I came up slowly, breaking the surface as quietly as I could. Treading water, I turned in a circle, my eyes scanning the yard for an intruder. At first, I saw nothing. And then I saw a pair of eyes, the moonlight caught in them just so.

Looking at me.

"I didn't know you were out here," the owner of those eyes said. "I should go."

My heart kept right on pounding, even once I realized the voice belonged to Dean. Now that my brain had identified him, I could make out a few more of his features. His hair hung in his face. His eyes—which I'd seen as a predator's a moment before—now just looked surprised.

Clearly, he hadn't expected anyone to be swimming at three in the morning.

"No," I said, my voice traveling along the surface of the water. "It's your yard, too. Stay."

I felt ridiculous for being so jumpy. This was a quiet, sleepy little town. The yard was fenced. No one knew what the FBI was training us to do. We weren't targets. This wasn't my dream.

I wasn't my mother.

For an elongated moment, I thought Dean would turn and walk away, but instead, he sat a few inches away from the edge of the pool. "What are you doing out here?"

For some reason, I felt compelled to tell him the truth. "I couldn't sleep."

Dean gazed out at the yard. "I stopped sleeping a long time ago. Most nights, I get three good hours, maybe four."

I'd given him a truth, and he'd given me one. We fell into silence then, him at the edge of the pool and me treading water at the center.

"It wasn't real, you know." He spoke to his hands, not to me.

"What wasn't real?"

"Today." Dean paused. "At the mall with Locke. Playing games in parking lots. That's not what this is."

In the scant light of the moon, his eyes looked so dark they were nearly black, and something about the way he was looking at me made me realize—he wasn't criticizing me.

He was trying to *protect* me.

"I know what this is," I said. I knew better than anyone. Turning away from him, I stared up at the sky, all too aware of the fact that he was staring at me.

"Briggs shouldn't have brought you here," he said finally. "This place will ruin you."

"Did it ruin Lia?" I asked. "Or Sloane?"

"They're not profilers."

"Did this place ruin *you*?"

Dean didn't pause, not even for a second. "There was nothing to ruin."

I swam over to the edge, right next to him. "You don't know me," I said, pulling myself out of the water. "I'm not scared of this place. I'm not afraid to learn how to think like a killer, and I am not afraid of *you*."

I wasn't even sure why I'd added on those last six words, but they were the ones that made his eyes flash. I was halfway to the house when I heard him stand up. I heard him walk across the grass to the tiny, shacklike pool house. I heard him throw a switch.

Suddenly, the yard wasn't dark anymore. It took me a moment to realize where the light was coming from. The pool was *glowing*. There was no other word for it. It looked like someone had splattered glow-in-the-dark paint across the edge. There was a drop of fluorescent color here, a drop there. Long streaks of it. Blobs. Four parallel smears across the tile on the side of the pool.

I glanced at Dean.

"Black light," he said, as if that were all the explanation I'd need.

I couldn't help myself. I moved closer. I squatted to get a better look. And that was when I saw the glow-in-the-dark outline of a body at the bottom of the pool.

"Her name was Amanda," Dean said.

I realized then what the smears and streaks of paint on the concrete and the side of the pool were supposed to be.

Blood.

The color had fooled me, even though the pattern was all too familiar.

"She was stabbed three times." Dean wouldn't look at me, wouldn't even look at the pool. "She cracked her head on the cement when she slipped in her own blood. And then he wrapped her fingers around her throat. He forced her upper body over the side of the pool."

I could see it happening, see the killer standing over a girl's body. She would have kicked. She would have clawed at his hands, tried to use the side of the pool for leverage.

"He held her under." Dean knelt next to the pool and demonstrated, acting out the motion. "He drowned her. And then he set her free." He let go of his imaginary prey and sent her off toward the center of the pool.

"This is a crime scene," I said finally. "One of the fake crime scenes that they use to test us, like the sets in the basement."

Dean stared out at the center of the pool, where the victim's body would have been. "It's not fake," he said finally. "It really happened. It just didn't happen here."

I reached out to touch Dean's shoulder. He shrugged off my touch, turning to face me, his body close to mine.

"Everything about this place—the house, the yard, the pool—was constructed with one thing in mind."

"Full immersion," I said, holding his gaze. "Like those schools where they only speak French."

Dean jerked his head toward the pool. "This isn't a language people should want to learn."

Normal people—that was what Dean meant. But I wasn't normal. I was a Natural. And this mock crime scene wasn't the worst thing I'd seen.

I turned to walk back to the house. I heard Dean walk across the lawn. I heard him flip the switch. And when I glanced back over my shoulder, the pool was just a pool. The yard was just a yard. And the outline of the body was gone.

overslept the next morning and woke up to the feeling that I was being watched.

"Knock, knock."

Based on the greeting—and the fact that the person speaking had opened my door, knocked on it, and said those words at the exact same time—I expected Lia. Instead, I opened my eyes to find Agent Locke standing in my doorway, a cup from Starbucks in one hand and car keys in the other.

I glanced over at Sloane's bed, but it was empty.

"Late night?" my newly acquired mentor asked, eyebrows arched. I thought of Dean and the pool and decided that was not an area of discussion I wanted to pursue.

"Really?" Agent Locke said, eyeing the look on my face. "I was just kidding, but you've got I-was-up-late-with-a-boy-last-night face. Maybe we should have some girl talk."

I didn't know what was worse, the fact that Locke thought my late night had something to do with a stupid teenage crush or the fact that she sounded suspiciously like my female cousins.

"No girl talk," I said. "As a general rule, ever."

Agent Locke nodded. "So noted." She eyed my pajamas, and then jerked her head toward the closet. "Get up. Get dressed." She tossed me the car keys. "I'll get Dean. You're driving."

I wasn't exactly happy when Agent Locke's directions ended up taking us right back to the mall—and specifically to Mrs. Fields cookies. After seeing the mocked-up blood spatter on the pool's edge the night before, profiling shoppers seemed senseless. It seemed silly.

If she makes us guess what kind of cookies people are going to order . . .

"Three and a half years ago, Sandy Harrison was here with her husband and their three children. Her husband took their eight-year-old son to the bookstore, and she was left with the two younger girls." Agent Locke said all of this in a perfectly normal voice. Not a single shopper turned to look at us, but her words froze me to the spot. "Sandy and the girls were in line for lemonade. Three-year-old Madelyn made a beeline for the cookies, and Sandy had to pull her back. It was Christmastime, and the mall was crammed full of people. Madelyn was desperately in need of a nap and on the verge of a meltdown. The line was moving. Sandy made it to the counter and turned to ask her older daughter, Annabelle, whether she wanted regular lemonade or pink."

I knew what was coming.

"Annabelle was gone."

It was easy to picture the mall at Christmastime, to see the young family splitting up, the father taking the son and the mother juggling two young girls. I saw the smaller one on the verge of a tantrum, saw the mother's attention diverted. I imagined her looking down and realizing that even though she'd just looked away for a few seconds, even though she was always *so* careful . . .

"Mall security was called immediately. Within half an hour, they'd alerted the police. They stopped traffic into and out of the mall. The FBI was called on board and we issued an AMBER Alert. If a child isn't recovered in the first twenty-four hours, then chances are good that he or she will never be recovered alive."

I swallowed hard. "Did you find her?"

"We did," Agent Locke replied. "The question is, would *you* have?" She let that sink in for a second, maybe two. "The first hour is the most crucial, and you've already lost that. The girl was missing for ninety-seven minutes before you even got the call. You need to figure out who took her and why. Most abductions are committed by family members, but her parents weren't divorced and there were no custody issues. You need to know this family's secrets. You need to know them inside and out—and you need to figure out how someone got that little girl out of this mall. What do you do?"

I looked around at the mall, at the people here. "Security footage?" I asked.

"Nothing," Locke said tersely. "There's no physical evidence, not even a scrap."

Dean spoke up. "She didn't cry." Agent Locke nodded, and he continued. "Even at Christmastime, even in a crowd, I'm not going to risk forcibly grabbing a kid whose mother is three feet away."

I couldn't quite bring myself to get in the abductor's head, so I did the next best thing. I got into Annabelle's. "I see someone. Maybe I know him. Maybe he has something I want. Or maybe he dropped something and I want to give it back." I paused. "I'm not the one crying and begging for cookies. I'm the older sister. I'm a good girl. I'm *mature* . . . so I follow him. Just to get a better look, just to hand something back to him, whatever. . . ." I paced out the steps. Five of them, and I was around the corner and facing a service door.

Obligingly, Dean went to open it, but it was locked.

"Maybe I work here," he said. "Maybe I've just stolen the access card. Either way, I'm prepared. I'm ready. Maybe I was just waiting for a child—any child—to take the bait."

"That's the question, isn't it?" Agent Locke said. "Was this a crime of opportunity or was the girl a specific target? To find her, you'd need to know."

I backed up and tried to play the scene all over again.

"What kind of person are you looking for?" Agent Locke asked. "Male? Female? What's the age range? Intelligence? Education?"

I looked at the cookie store, then the service door, then at Dean. This was what he was talking about the night before. This was the job.

All business, I turned back to Agent Locke. "Exactly how old was the girl?"

CHAPTER 14

"**L**ocke working you too hard?" Michael swooped in on me at breakfast, a habit of his, and one I'd grown to look forward to in the past week. Every day, Agent Locke showed up with a new challenge, and every day, I solved it. With Dean.

Sometimes, it felt like mornings with Michael were my only real break.

"Some of us like working hard," I told him.

"As opposed to those of us who are the entitled product of an oh-so-privileged upbringing?" Michael asked, wiggling his eyebrows.

"That wasn't what I meant."

He leaned over and tweaked my ponytail. "Likely story, Colorado."

"Do you really hate it here?" I asked. I couldn't tell if he legitimately disliked the program or if the attitude was for show. The biggest thing I'd figured out about Michael in the past week was that there was a very good chance that he'd been wearing masks for longer than he'd been working for the FBI—pretending to be something he wasn't was second nature.

"Let's just say that I have the rare ability to be dissatisfied wherever I am," Michael said, "although I'm starting to think this place has its perks." This time, instead of messing with my ponytail, he pushed a stray piece of hair out of my face.

"Cassie." Dean's voice took me by surprise, and I jumped. "Locke's here."

"All work and no play," Michael whispered.

I ignored him—and went to work.

"One. Two. Three." Agent Locke set the pictures down one at a time. "Four, five, six, and seven."

Two rows of pictures—three in one row and four in the other—stared up at me from the kitchen table. Each picture contained a body: glassy eyes, limbs splayed every which way.

"Am I interrupting?"

Locke, Dean, and I turned to see Judd in the doorway. "Yes," Locke said with a smile. "You are. What can we do for you, Judd?"

The older man bit back a smile of his own. "You, young lady, can point me in Briggs's direction."

"Briggs is out doing some legwork on a case," Locke replied. "It's just me today."

Judd was silent for a moment. His eyes fell on the pictures on the kitchen table, and he raised an eyebrow at Locke. "Clean up when you're done."

With that, Judd left us to our own devices, and I turned my attention back to the photographs. The three on the top row featured women lying lifeless on pavement. The four on the bottom were indoors: two on beds, one on the kitchen floor, one in a bathtub. Three of the victims had been stabbed. Two had been shot. One had been bludgeoned, and one had been strangled.

I forced myself to stare at the pictures. If I blinked, if I turned away, if I flinched, I might not be able to look back. Beside me, Dean was looking at the pictures, too. He scanned them, left to right, up and down, like he was taking inventory, like the bodies in these pictures hadn't ever been people: somebody's mother, somebody's love.

"Seven bodies," Agent Locke said. "Five killers. Three of these women were killed by the same man. The remaining four were the work of four different killers." Agent Locke tapped lightly on the top of each photo, bringing my eyes from one to the next. "Different victims, different locations, different weapons. What's significant? What's not? As profilers, a large part of our job is identifying patterns. There are millions of unsolved cases out there. How do you know if the killer you're tracking is responsible for any of them?"

I could never tell when Agent Locke was asking a rhetorical question and when she expected an answer. A few seconds of keeping my mouth shut told me that this was an instance of the first.

Agent Locke turned to Dean. "Care to explain to Cassie the difference between a killer's MO and their signature?"

Dean tore his attention away from the photos and forced himself to look at me. Studying mutilated bodies was routine. Talking to me—apparently, *that* was hard.

"MO stands for *modus operandi*," he said, and that's as far as he got before he shifted his gaze from my face to a spot just over my left shoulder. "Mode of operation. It refers to the method used by the killer. Location, weapon, how they pick victims, how they subdue them—that's a killer's MO."

He looked down at his hands, and I looked at them, too. His palms were calloused, his fingernails short and uneven. A thin white scar snaked its way from the base of his right thumb to the outside of his wrist.

"A killer's MO can change," Dean continued, and I tried to focus on his words instead of his scar. "An UNSUB might start off killing his victims quickly. He's not sure he'll be able to get away with it, but with time and experience, a lot of UNSUBs develop ways to savor the kill. Some killers escalate—taking more chances, spacing their kills closer together."

Dean closed his eyes for a split second before opening them again. "Anything about an UNSUB's MO is subject to change, so while it can be *informative* to track the MO, it's not exactly bulletproof." Dean fingered the closest picture again. "That's where their signature comes in."

Agent Locke took up the slack in the explanation. "An UNSUB's MO includes all of the elements *necessary* to commit a crime and evade capture. As a killer, you *have* to select a victim, you *have* to have a means of executing the crime unnoticed, you *have* to have either physical prowess or some kind of weapon to kill them with. You *have* to dispose of the body in some way."

Agent Locke pointed to the picture that had captured Dean's attention.

"But after you stab someone in the back, you don't *have* to roll them over and pose their arms, palms up at their sides." She stopped pointing, but kept talking—about other killers, other things that she'd seen in her work with the FBI. "You don't *have* to kiss their foreheads or cut off their lips or leave a piece of origami next to the body."

Agent Locke's expression was serious, but nowhere near as detached as Dean's. She'd been doing this job for a while, but it still got to her—the way it would probably always get to me. "Collectively, we refer to these extra actions—and what they tell us about the UNSUB—as a *signature*. An UNSUB's signature tells us something about his or her underlying psychology: fantasies, deep-seated needs, emotions."

Dean looked down at his hands. "Those needs, those fantasies, those emotions," he said, "they don't change. A killer can switch weapons, they can start killing on a quicker schedule, they can change venues, they can start targeting a different class of victims—but their signature stays the same."

I turned my attention back to the pictures. Three of the women had been stabbed: two in back alleys, one in her own kitchen. The woman in the kitchen had fought; from the looks of the pictures, the other two had never had a chance.

"These two," I said, pulling out the first two stabbing pictures. "The killer surprised them. You said the UNSUB stabbed this one from behind." I indicated the girl on the left. "After she was dead—or close enough to it that she couldn't put up much of a fight—he turned her over. So she could see him."

This was what Agent Locke was talking about when she used the phrase *deep-seated need*. The killer had attacked this girl from behind, but it was important to him—for whatever reason—that she see his face and that he see hers.

"Don't say *he*," Dean said. He shifted, and suddenly, I could feel the heat from his body. "Say *you*, Cassie. Or say *I*."

"Fine," I said. I stopped talking about the killer—and started talking *to* him. "You want them to see you. You want to stand over them. And as they lie there dying, or maybe even after they're dead, you can't help but touch them. You straighten their clothes. You lay their arms out to the side." I stared at the picture of the girl he'd attacked from behind, and something else struck me about it. "You think they're beautiful, but girls like that, women like that, they never even see you." I paused. "So you *make them* see you."

I looked at the next picture: another woman, stabbed and found dead on the pavement. Like the first, she'd been chosen for convenience. But according to the notes on the picture, she hadn't been stabbed from behind.

"It wasn't enough," I said. "Turning her over after she died, it wasn't enough. So you took the next one from the front."

Like the first victim, this one had been laid carefully on her back, her hair fanned around her face in an unnatural halo. Without even thinking about it, I took the third picture on the top row—a gunshot victim who'd died running—and set it aside. That wasn't the work of the same UNSUB. It was quick and clean, and there wasn't a whiff of desire about it.

Turning my attention to the bottom row of pictures, I scanned them, trying to keep my emotions in check the way Dean did. One of these four women had been killed by the same UNSUB as the first two. The easy answer—and the wrong one—would have been the third stabbing victim, but she'd been stabbed in the kitchen, with a knife from her own drawer. She'd fought, she'd died bloody, and the killer had left her there, her skirt on sideways, her body contorted.

You need to see them, I told the killer silently, picturing his silhouette in my mind. *You need them to see you. They need to be beautiful.*

This third victim had been killed after the first two. The UNSUB's MO had changed: different weapon, different location. But deep down, the killer hadn't changed. He was still the same person with the same sick underlying needs.

Every time you kill, you need more. You need to be better. She *needs to be better. Killing women on the street wasn't enough anymore. You didn't want a quickie in a back alley. You wanted a relationship. A woman. A home.*

I zeroed in on the two women who'd been killed in their bedrooms. Both had been found lying on their beds. One had been shot. The other had been strangled.

You catch her at night. In her house. In her bedroom. She doesn't look through you now, does she? She's not too good for you now.

I tried to imagine the UNSUB shooting a woman, but the math on that one just did not compute.

You want her to see you. You want to touch her. You want to feel the life going out of her, little by little.

"This was the last one," I said, pointing to the woman who'd been strangled in her own bed. "Different MO. Same signature."

This woman had died watching him, and he'd posed her,

propped her head up on a pillow, fanning her brown hair out around her death-still face.

Suddenly, I was nauseous. It wasn't just what had been done to these women. It was that for a moment, I'd connected with the person who'd done it. I'd *understood*.

I felt a hand, warm and steady, on the back of my neck. Dean.

"You're fine," he said. "It'll pass."

This from the boy who'd never wanted me to go to the place I'd just gone.

"Just breathe," he told me, dark eyes making a careful study of mine. I returned the favor, concentrating on his face—here, now, this moment, nothing else.

"You okay, Cass?" Agent Locke sounded worried in spite of herself. I could practically see her wondering if she'd pushed me too far, too fast.

"I'm fine," I said.

"Liar." Lia strolled into the kitchen like a model on a catwalk, but for once, I was glad for the distraction.

"Okay," I said, amending my previous statement. "I'm not fine, but I will be." I turned around and met Lia's eyes. "Satisfied?"

She smiled. "Delighted."

Agent Locke cleared her throat and adopted a stern expression that reminded me of Agent Briggs. "We're still working here, Lia."

Lia looked at me, then at Dean, who dropped his hands to his side. "No," she said. "You're not."

I wasn't sure if Lia was calling Locke out on a lie or telling the agent to back off. I also wasn't sure whether she was doing it for me—or for Dean.

"Fine," Agent Locke capitulated. "My brilliant lecture on the difference between organized and disorganized killers can wait until tomorrow." Her phone vibrated. She picked it up, glanced at the screen for a few seconds, and then corrected herself. "And by 'tomorrow,'" she said, "I mean Monday. Have a good weekend."

"Somebody has a case," Lia said, her eyes lighting up.

"Somebody has to jet," Agent Locke replied. "No rest for the wicked, and as much as I'd love to take a human lie detector with me to a crime scene, Lia, that's not what this program is. You know that."

I'd gotten nauseous over pictures, long-dead women, and a killer who'd already been convicted. Locke was talking about an active crime scene.

A fresh body.

"You're right," Dean said, stepping in between Lia and Locke. "That's not what this program is," he told the agent, and even from behind, I could picture the look in his eyes— intense and full of warning. "Not anymore."

YOU

You're getting sloppy, killing so close to home, leaving the bodies spread throughout the back streets of the capital, like Hansel and Gretel dropping more and more bread crumbs the farther into the forest they go.

But from the moment you first laid eyes on her, it's been harder to push back the desire to kill, harder to remember why you make it a point not to play in your own backyard.

Maybe this is the way it's supposed to be. Maybe it's fate.

Time to finish what you started.

Time to get their attention.

Time to come home.

CHAPTER 15

I woke up on Saturday at noon to two sounds: the shuffling of cards and the faint, high-pitched whir of metal on metal. I opened my eyes and turned over onto my side. Sloane was sitting cross-legged on her bed, a mug in one hand and the other dealing out cards: seven columns, a different number of cards in each one, all of them facedown.

"What are you doing?" I asked.

Sloane stared at the backs of the cards for a moment and then picked one up and moved it. "Solitaire," she said.

"But all of the cards are facedown."

"Yes." Sloane took a sip from her mug.

"How can you play Solitaire if all of the cards are facedown?"

Sloane shrugged. "How can you play with some of them faceup?"

"Sloane is something of a card shark. Briggs found her in Vegas." Lia stuck her head out of the closet. "If she skims the deck once, she can more or less track the cards, even once they're shuffled."

I registered the fact that Lia was in our closet. *Metal on metal,* I thought. *Metal hangers sliding across a metal rack.*

"Hey," I said, taking a better look at Lia's current attire. "That's my dress."

"Mine now." Lia smiled. "Didn't the FBI warn you that I have sticky fingers? Kleptomania, pathological lying—it's all the same, really."

I thought Lia was joking, but I couldn't be sure.

"Kidding," she confirmed after a few seconds. "About the kleptomania, not about the fact that I have no intention of giving this dress back. Honestly, *Sloane* is the klepto in this house, but this really is more my color than yours."

I turned to Sloane, who'd ratcheted the speed of her game up a notch—or three.

"Sloane," I said.

"Yes?"

"Why is Lia poking around in our closet?"

Sloane looked up, but didn't stop playing. "Motivation is really more your domain than mine. I find most people somewhat bewildering."

I rephrased the question. "Why would you *let* Lia poke around in our closet?"

"Oh," Sloane said, once she took my meaning. "She brought a bribe."

"Bribe?" I asked. And that was when I realized what, exactly, was in Sloane's mug.

"You brought her coffee?"

Lia smoothed a hand over the front of *my* dress. "Guilty as charged."

Sloane on coffee was a bit like an auctioneer on speed. The numbers poured out of her mouth rapid-fire, a statistic for every occasion. For *eight hours.*

"Sixteen percent of American men have blue eyes," she informed me blithely. "But over forty percent of male TV doctors do."

Watching TV with a hyped-up statistician would have been challenging enough, but Sloane wasn't the only one who'd followed me to the media room after dinner.

"Her mouth says, *I love you, Darren,* but her posture says, *I can't believe the writers are doing this to my character—she would never get involved with this schmuck!*" Michael popped a piece of popcorn into his mouth.

"Do you mind?" I asked him, gesturing toward the screen. He grinned. "Not at all."

I tried to tune the two of them out, but the effort was futile. I couldn't get lost in the medical melodrama any more than they could, because all I could think—over and over again—was that Dr. Darren the Schmuck's BPE simply did *not* add up.

"We could switch to reality TV," Michael suggested.

"Roughly one percent of the population are considered to be psychopaths," Sloane announced. "Recent estimates suggest that over fourteen percent of reality television stars are."

"Whose estimates?" Michael asked.

Sloane smiled like a Cheshire cat. "Mine."

Michael put his hands behind his head and leaned back. "Forget studying killers. Let's arrest fourteen percent of all reality television stars and call it a day."

Sloane slouched in her chair and toyed with the end of her ponytail. "Being a psychopath isn't a crime," she said.

"Are you defending psychopaths?" Michael asked, arching one eyebrow to ridiculous heights. "This is why we don't give you coffee."

"Hey," Sloane said defensively, "I'm just saying that statistically, a psychopath is more likely to end up as a CEO than a serial killer."

"Ahem." Lia was the only person I knew who would actually say the word *ahem* to announce her presence. Once she had our attention, she looked at each one of us in turn. "Judd just left for a night on the town with an old friend. We have the house to ourselves." She clasped her hands together in front of her body. "Living room. Fifteen minutes. Come prepared."

"Prepared for what?" I asked, but before the question had fully exited my mouth, she was gone.

"That probably does not bode well." Michael's words didn't sound much like a complaint. He stood. "I'll see you ladies in fifteen."

As I watched him walk out the door, I couldn't help thinking that I'd spent most of my life as an observer, and Lia was the type to pull people off the sidelines.

"Any guesses what we're getting ourselves into?" I asked Sloane.

"Based on previous experience," Sloane replied, "my guess would be *trouble*."

CHAPTER 16

Michael and Dean were already in the living room when Sloane and I arrived. In the past fourteen minutes, my blond companion had quieted, like the Energizer Bunny powering down. She took a seat on the sofa next to Michael. I sat down next to her. Across from us, Dean was sitting on the edge of the fireplace, his gaze locked on the floor, hair in his face.

Sofa, chairs, pillows, rug, I thought. *And he chooses to sit on stone.*

I flashed back to the first time I'd seen him, lifting weights and pushing his body to the brink. My very first impression had been that he was punishing himself.

"Glad to see you all made it." Lia didn't just walk into a room; she made an entrance. All eyes on her, she sank to the floor and stretched her legs out, crossing her feet at the ankles and spreading *my* dress out around her. "For your entertainment this evening: Truth or Dare." She paused, raking her eyes over the rest of us. "Any objections?"

Dean opened his mouth.

"No," Lia told him.

"You asked for objections," Dean said.

Lia shook her head. "You don't get to object."

"Do I?" Michael asked.

Lia considered the question. "Do you want to?"

Michael glanced at me, then back at Lia. "Not particularly."

"Then, yes," Lia replied. "You do."

Beside me, Sloane raised her hand.

"Yes, Sloane?" Lia said pleasantly. Apparently, she wasn't concerned that our resident numbers girl might object.

"I'm familiar with the gist of the game, but I'm unclear on one thing." Sloane's eyes gleamed. "How do you win?"

Michael grinned. "You have to love a girl with a competitive streak."

"You don't *win* Truth or Dare," I said. In fact, I deeply suspected this was the kind of game that everybody lost.

"Is that an objection?" Lia asked.

From across the room, Dean was telegraphing the words *SAY YES* to me, as clearly as if he'd hired a plane to write them in the sky. And if I'd been in a room with any other teenagers on the planet, I would have. But I was in a room with Michael, who I couldn't quite profile, and Dean, who'd said the other day that Naturals didn't work on active cases *anymore.* I had questions, and this was the only way I was going to get to ask them.

"No," I told Lia. "That wasn't an objection. Let's play."

A slow smile spread across Lia's face. Dean banged his head back against the fireplace.

"Can I go first?" Sloane asked.

"Sure," Lia replied smoothly. "Truth or dare, Sloane?"

Sloane gave her a look. "That's not what I meant."

Lia shrugged. "Truth. Or. Dare."

"Truth."

In a normal game of Truth or Dare, that would have been the safer option—because if the question was too embarrassing, you could always lie. With Lia in the room, that was impossible.

"Do you know who your father is?"

Lia's question took me completely off guard. I'd spent most of my life not knowing who my own father was, but couldn't imagine being forced to admit that in front of a crowd. Lia seemed fond of Sloane, more or less, but clearly, in Truth or Dare, the kid gloves came off.

Sloane met Lia's eyes, unfazed. "Yes," she said. "I do."

"A swing and a miss," Michael murmured. Lia gave him a dirty look.

"Your turn," she told Sloane, and from the look on her face, I guessed she was bracing herself for payback—but Sloane turned to me.

"Cassie. Truth or dare?"

I tried to imagine what kind of dare Sloane might come up with, but drew a blank.

"Statistically, the most common dares involve eating unpleasant food, making prank phone calls, kissing another player, licking something unsanitary, and nudity," Sloane said helpfully.

"Truth."

Sloane was silent for several seconds. "How many people do you love?"

The question seemed harmless enough until I started thinking about my answer. Sloane's blue eyes searched mine, and I got the distinct feeling that she wasn't asking because she thought it would be amusing to hear my answer.

She was asking because she needed data points to compare to her own.

"How many people do I love?" I repeated. "Like . . . love how?"

I'd never been in love, so if she was talking about romance, the answer was easy.

"How many people do you love, total?" Sloane said. "Summing across familial, romantic, and all other variations."

I wanted to just choose a number at random. Five sounded good. Or ten. *Too many to count* sounded better, but Lia was watching me, very still.

I'd loved my mother. That much was easy. And Nonna

and my father and the rest—I loved them. Didn't I? They were my family. They loved me. Just because I wasn't showy about it didn't mean that I didn't love them back. I'd done what I could to make them happy. I tried not to hurt them.

But did I really love them, the way I'd loved my mom? *Could* I love anyone like that again?

"One." I barely managed to get the word out of my mouth. I stared at Lia, hoping she'd tell me that wasn't true, that losing my mom hadn't broken something inside of me and I wasn't destined to spend the rest of my life two shades removed from the kind of love that the rest of my family felt for me.

Lia held my gaze for a few seconds, then shrugged. "Your turn, Cassie."

I tried to remember why I'd thought playing this game was a good idea. "Michael," I said finally. "Truth or dare?"

There were so many things I wanted to ask him—what he really thought of the program, what his father was like, beyond the issue of tax fraud, whether there had ever been more to his relationship with Lia than trading verbal barbs. But I didn't get a chance to ask any of those questions, because Michael leaned forward in his seat, his eyes gleaming. "Dare."

Of course he wasn't going to let me dig around in his brain. Of course he was going to make me issue the first dare of the game. I racked my brain for something that didn't sound lame, but also didn't involve kissing, nudity, or anything that might give Michael an excuse for trouble.

"Hit me with your best shot, Colorado." Michael was enjoying this way too much. I had a feeling he was hoping that I would dare him to do something a little bit dangerous, something that would get his adrenaline pumping.

Something Briggs would disapprove of.

"I dare you . . ." I said the words slowly, hoping an answer would present itself. ". . . to dance ballet."

Even I wasn't sure where that came from.

"What?" Michael said. Clearly, he'd been expecting something a little more exciting, or at the very least risqué.

"Ballet," I repeated. "Right there." I pointed to the center of the rug. "Dance."

Lia started cracking up. Even Dean bit back a smile.

"Ballet is a tradition of performance body movement hailing back to the early Renaissance," Sloane said helpfully. "It is particularly popular in Russia, France, Italy, England, and the United States."

Michael stopped her before she could orate an entire history of the art. "I've got this," he said. And then, a solemn expression on his face, he stood up, he walked to the center of the room, and he struck a pose.

I'd seen Michael do smooth. I'd seen him do suave. I'd felt him push a piece of hair out of my face—but *this*. This was really something. He stood on his tippy-toes. He twirled in a circle. He bent his legs and stuck out his butt. But the best thing was the look in his eyes: cold, steely determination.

He capped the performance off with a curtsy.

"Very nice," I said between hysterical giggles. He sank back onto the sofa and then turned dagger eyes on Lia.

"Truth or dare."

Not surprisingly, Lia chose truth. Of all of us, she was probably the only one here who could lie and get away with it.

Michael smiled, as genial as Lia had been when she'd started this whole thing. "What's your real name?"

For a few brief seconds, vulnerability and irritation passed over Lia's features in quick succession.

"Your name isn't Lia?" Sloane sounded strangely hurt at the idea that Lia might have lied about something as simple and basic as her own name.

"Yes," Lia told her. "It is."

Michael stared at Lia, raising his eyebrows ever so slightly.

"But once upon a time," Lia said, sounding less and less like herself with every word, "my name used to be Sadie."

Lia's answer filled my mind with questions. I tried to picture her as a Sadie. Had she shed her old name as easily as she changed clothes? Why had she changed it? How had Michael known?

"Truth or dare . . ." Lia dragged her eyes across each of us, one by one, and I sensed something dark slowly unfurling inside of her. This wasn't going to end well.

"Cassie."

It didn't seem fair that it was my turn again already, when Dean had yet to go, but I stepped up to the plate.

"Dare." I don't know what possessed me to choose that option, other than the fact that the look on Lia's face convinced me that she'd make Sloane's question look about as personal as an inquiry about the weather.

Lia beamed at me, and then beamed at Michael. *Payback.*

"I dare you," Lia said, relishing each and every word, "to kiss Dean."

Dean reacted to that sentence like he'd been electrocuted. He sat straight up. "Lia," he said sharply. "No."

"Oh, come now, Dean," Lia cajoled. "It's Truth or Dare. Take one for the team." Without waiting for his reply, she turned back to me. "Kiss him, Cassie."

I didn't know what was worse, Dean's objection to the idea of being forced to kiss me or the sudden realization that my body *didn't* object to the idea of kissing him. I thought of our lessons with Locke, the feel of his hand on the back of my neck. . . .

Lia watched me expectantly, but Michael's eyes were the ones I felt on my face as I crossed the room to stand in front of Dean.

I didn't have to do this.

I could say no.

Dean looked up at me, and for a split second, I saw

something other than deadly neutrality on his face. His eyes softened. His lips parted, like there was something he wanted to say.

I knelt next to the fireplace. I put one hand on his cheek, and I brought my lips to his. It was a friendly kiss. A European hello. Our mouths only touched for a second—but I felt it, electric, all the way to my toes.

I pulled back, unable to force my eyes away from his lips as I did. For a few seconds, we just stayed there, staring at each other: him on the fireplace and me kneeling on the rug.

"Your turn, Cassie." Lia sounded pretty darned satisfied with herself.

I forced myself to stand up and walk back to the sofa. I sat down, still able to feel the ghost of Dean's lips on mine. "Truth or dare, Dean?"

It was only fair: he was the sole person present who hadn't been in the hot seat yet. For a second, I thought he might refuse and call an end to this game, but he didn't.

"Truth."

This was the opportunity Michael hadn't given me. There were so many things I wanted to know. I concentrated on that, instead of what had passed between us a moment before.

"The other day, when Locke said she couldn't take Lia to the crime scene, you said that wasn't what the program was *anymore*." I paused. "What did you mean?"

Dean nodded, as if that were a perfectly reasonable question to ask after you'd kissed a person. "I was the first one," he said. "Before there was a program, before they started using the term *Naturals*, it was just Briggs and me. I didn't live with Judd. The FBI brass didn't know about me. Briggs brought me questions. I gave him answers."

"Questions about killers." I wasn't allowed a follow-up question, so I phrased it as a statement. Dean nodded. Lia cut in, breaking off all conversation.

"He was twelve," she said, clipping the words. "Your turn, Dean."

"Cassie," Dean said. That was it—no "truth or dare." Just my name.

Beside me, Michael's jaw clenched. Lia's payback had hit its target—and then some.

"Truth," I said, trying not to dwell on Michael's reaction or what it might mean.

"Why did you come here?" Dean asked, looking at Lia, at his own hands, at anything but me. "Why join this program at all?"

There were a lot of answers to that question that would have been technically true. I could have said that I wanted to help people. I could have said that I'd always known that I'd never quite fit in the regular world. But I didn't.

"My mother was murdered." I cleared my throat, trying to say the words like they were just any other words. "Five years ago. Based on the blood spatter, they think she was stabbed. Repeatedly. The police never found her body, but there was enough blood that they don't think she could have survived. I used to think that maybe she had. I don't anymore."

Dean didn't react visibly to that confession—but Lia went unnaturally still, and Sloane's mouth dropped open as she averted her eyes. Michael had known about my mother, but I'd never said a word to any of the others.

Truth or dare, Dean. I wanted to say the words, but I couldn't keep asking Dean questions. Already, we'd kept this game between the two of us for too long. "Truth or dare, Lia?"

"Truth." Lia said the word like a challenge. I asked her whether she was messy or neat. She lowered her chin, raised her eyebrows, and stared at me.

"Seriously," she said. "That's your question?"

"That's my question," I confirmed.

"I'm a mess," she said. "By *every* sense of the word." She didn't give me time to meditate on the fact that I'd pegged her right before she targeted Michael for the next round. I expected him to pick dare again, but he didn't.

"Truth."

Lia ran dainty hands over her dress. She gave him her most wide-eyed, innocent look. Then she asked him if he was jealous when I kissed Dean. Michael didn't bat an eye, but I thought Dean might actually throttle Lia.

"I don't get jealous," Michael said. "I get even."

No one was surprised when Michael aimed the next round at Dean.

"Truth or dare, Dean?"

"Truth." Dean's eyes narrowed, and I remembered Lia saying that if Dean had a temper, Michael would have been dead by now. I waited, my stomach heavy and my throat dry, for Michael to ask Dean something horrible.

But he didn't.

"Have you ever seen *The Bad Seed*?" he inquired politely. "The movie."

A muscle in Dean's jaw twitched. "No."

Michael grinned. "I have."

Dean stood up. "I'm done here."

"Dean—" Lia's tone was halfway between mulish and wheedling, but he silenced her with a look. Two seconds later, he was stalking out of the room, and a few seconds after that, I heard the front door open, then slam.

Dean was gone—and a person didn't have to be an emotion reader to see the look of satisfaction on Michael's face.

YOU

Every hour, every day, you think about The Girl. But it's not time for the grand finale. Not yet. Instead, you find another toy at a little shop in Dupont Circle. You've had your eye on her for a while, but resisted the urge to add her to your collection. She was too close to home, in an area that was too densely populated.

*But right now, the so-called Madame Selene is just what you need. Bodies are bodies, but a palm reader—there's a certain poetry to that. A message you want—need—*have *to send. It would be simpler to kill her in the shop, to drive a knife through each palm and leave her body on display, but you've worked so hard this week.*

You deserve a little treat.

Taking her is easy. You're a ghost. A stranger with candy. A sympathetic ear. When Madame Selene wakes up in the warehouse, she won't believe that you're the one who's done this to her.

Not at first.

But eventually, she'll see.

You smile, thinking about the inevitability of it all. You touch the tips of her brown hair and pick up the handy box of Red Dye Number 12. You hum under your breath, a children's song that takes you back to the beginning, back to the first.

The palm reader's eyes flicker open. Her hands are bound. She sees you. Then she sees the hair dye, the knife in your left hand, and she realizes—

You are the monster.

And this time, you deserve to take things slow.

CHAPTER 17

When Agent Locke showed up Monday morning, she had dark circles under her eyes. Belatedly, I remembered that while we'd been watching TV and playing Truth or Dare, she and Briggs had been out working a case. A real case, with real stakes.

A real killer.

For a long time, Locke didn't say anything. "Briggs and I hit a brick wall this weekend," she said finally. "We've got three bodies, and the killer is escalating." She ran a hand through hair that looked like it had been only haphazardly brushed. "That's not your problem. It's mine, but this case has reminded me that the UNSUB is only half the story. Dean, what can you tell Cassie about victimology?"

Dean stared holes in the countertop. I hadn't seen him

since Truth or Dare, but it was like nothing had changed between us, like we'd never kissed.

"Most killers have a type," he said. "Sometimes, it's a physical type. For others, it may be a matter of convenience— maybe you focus on hikers, because no one reports them missing for a few days, or students, because it's easy to get ahold of their class schedules."

Agent Locke nodded. "Occasionally the victims may be serving as a substitute for someone in the UNSUB's life. Some killers kill their first girlfriend or their wife or their mother, over and over again."

"The other thing victimology tells us," Dean continued, flicking his eyes over to Agent Locke, "is how the victim would have reacted to being abducted or attacked. If you're a killer . . ." He paused, searching for the right words. "There's a give-and-take between you and the people you kill. You choose them. You trap them. Maybe they fight. Maybe they run. Some try to reason with you, some say things that set you off. Either way, you react."

"We don't have the luxury of knowing every last detail about the UNSUB's personality," Agent Locke cut in, "but the victim's personality and behavior account for half of the crime scene."

The moment I heard the phrase *crime scene*, I flashed back to opening the door to my mother's dressing room.

I'd always thought that I knew so little about what had happened that day. By the time I'd gotten back to the dressing room, the killer was gone. My mother was gone. There was so much blood. . . .

Victimology, I reminded myself. I knew my mother. She would have fought—nail-scratching, breaking-lamps-over-his-head, struggling-for-the-knife *fought*. And there were only two things that could have stopped her: dying or the realization that I was due back in the room at any second.

What if she went with him? The police had assumed she was dead—or at the very least unconscious—when the UNSUB had removed her from the room. But my mother wasn't a small woman, and the dressing room was on the second floor of the theater. Under normal circumstance, my mother wouldn't have just let a killer waltz her out the door—but she might have done anything to keep her assailant away from me.

"Cassie?" Agent Locke said, snapping me back to the present.

"Right," I said.

She narrowed her eyes. "Right what?"

"Sorry," I told Locke. "Could you repeat what you just said?"

She gave me a long, appraising look, then repeated herself. "I said that walking through a crime scene from a victim's perspective can tell you a lot about the killer. Say you go into a victim's house and you find out that she compulsively writes to-do lists, color-codes her clothes, and has a pet fish. This woman is the third victim, but she's the only one of the three who doesn't have defensive wounds. The killer normally keeps his victims alive for days, but this woman was killed by a strong blow to the head on the day she was taken. Her blouse was buttoned crookedly when they found her."

Putting myself into the killer's head, I could imagine him taking women. Playing with them. So why would he let this one off easy? Why end his game early, when she showed no signs of fighting back?

Because she showed no signs of fighting back.

I switched perspectives, imagining myself as the victim. *I'm organized, orderly, and type A in the extreme. I want a pet, but can't bring myself to get one that would actually disrupt my life, so I settle for a fish instead. Maybe I've read about the previous murders in the paper. Maybe I know how things end for the women who fought back.*

So maybe I don't fight back. Not physically.

The things Locke had told me about the victim said that she was a woman who liked to stay in control. She would have tried reasoning with her killer. She would have resisted his attempts to control her. She might have even tried to manipulate him. And if she'd succeeded, even for an instant . . .

"The UNSUB killed the others for fun," I said, "but he killed her in a fit of rage."

Their interaction would have been a game of control for him, too—and she was just enough of a control freak to disrupt that.

"And?" Agent Locke prompted.

I drew a blank.

"He buttoned her shirt," Dean said. "If she'd buttoned it, it wouldn't have been crooked."

That observation sent my mind whirring. If he'd killed her in a rage, why would he have dressed her afterward? If he'd *un*dressed her, I could understand it—the final humiliation, the final assertion of control.

You know her, I thought.

"The UNSUB's first two victims were chosen randomly." Agent Locke met my eyes, and for a second, it felt like she was reading my mind. "We assumed the third victim was as well. We were wrong." Locke rocked back on her heels. "That's why you need both sides of the coin. Checks and balances, victims and UNSUBs—because you'll always be wrong about something. You'll always miss something. What if there's a personal connection? What if the UNSUB is older than you thought? What if *he* is a *she*? What if there are two UNSUBs working as a pair? What if the killer is just a kid himself?"

I knew suddenly that we weren't talking about the type A woman and the man who'd killed her anymore. We were talking about the doubts plaguing Locke *right now,* the assumptions she'd made on her current case. We were talking about an UNSUB that Locke and Briggs hadn't been able to catch.

"Ninety percent of all serial killers are male." Sloane announced her presence, then walked up to join us. "Seventy-six percent are American, with a substantial percentage of serial murders concentrated in California, Texas, New York, and Illinois. The vast majority of serial killers are Caucasian, and over eighty-nine percent of victims of serial crimes are Caucasian as well."

I could not help noticing that she spoke significantly slower when not under the influence of caffeine.

Briggs followed Sloane into the room. "Lacey." He got Agent Locke's attention. "I just got a call from Starmans. We have body number four."

Thinking about those words—and what they meant—felt like eavesdropping, but I couldn't help myself. Another body. Another person, dead.

Locke clenched her jaw. "Same profile?" she asked Briggs.

Briggs gave a brisk, slight nod. "A palm reader in Dupont Circle. And the national database search we ran came back with more than one match for our killer's MO."

What MO? I couldn't shake the question, any more than I could stop wondering who this new victim was, if she'd had a family, who had told them that she was dead.

"That bad?" Locke asked, reading Briggs's face. I wished

Michael were there to help me do the same. This case was none of my business—but I wanted to know.

"We should talk elsewhere," Briggs said.

Elsewhere. As in somewhere that Sloane, Dean, and I weren't.

"You didn't have trouble coming to Dean for advice when he was *twelve*," I said, unable to stop myself. "Why stop now?"

Briggs's eyes darted over to Dean, who met his gaze without blinking. Clearly, that wasn't information Dean was supposed to share with the rest of us—but just as clearly, Dean wasn't going to look away first.

"The flower beds could use some weeding." Judd broke the tension, coming into the room to stand between Briggs and Dean. "If you're done with the kids for a bit, I can put them to work. Might be good for them to get their hands dirty, get some sun."

Judd directed those words at Agent Briggs, but Locke was the one who replied. "It's fine, Judd." She glanced first at Dean, then at me. "They can stay. Briggs, you were saying the database turned up more than one case with the same MO?"

For a moment, Briggs looked like he might argue with Locke about letting us stay, but she just stood there, stubbornly waiting him out.

Briggs gave in first. "Our database search returned three

cases consistent with our killer's MO in the past nine months," he said, clipping each word. "New Orleans, Los Angeles, and American Falls."

"Illinois?" Locke asked.

Briggs shook his head. "Idaho."

I processed that information. If the cases Briggs was talking about were related, we were dealing with a killer who'd crossed state lines and had been killing for the better part of a year.

"My go bag is in the car," Locke said, and suddenly, I remembered—*we* weren't dealing with anything. Locke hadn't let Briggs shuffle the three of us out of the room, but at the end of the day, this wasn't a training exercise, and it wasn't *my* case, or even *ours*.

It was *theirs*.

"We leave at sixteen hundred hours." Briggs straightened his tie. "I left work for Lia, Michael, and Sloane. Locke, do you have anything for Cassie and Dean—besides weeding the flower beds?" he added with a glance at Judd.

"I'm not leaving them a cold case." Locke turned to me, almost apologetically. "You have an incredible amount of raw talent, Cass, but you've spent too much time in the real world and not enough in ours. Not yet."

"She can handle anything you throw at her."

I looked at Dean, surprised. He was the last person I expected to be making this argument on my behalf.

"Thank you for that glowing endorsement, Dean," Locke said, "but I'm not going to rush this. Not with her." She paused. "Library," she told me. "Third shelf from the left. There's a series of blue binders. Prison interviews. Make your way through those, and we'll talk about getting you started on cold cases when I get back."

"I don't think that's a good idea." Dean's voice was curiously flat. Locke shrugged.

"You're the one who said she was ready."

CHAPTER 18

That night, when I snuck out to the pool for a midnight swim, Dean wasn't the one who joined me.

"I would have pegged you for a no-nonsense one-piece," Michael said as I came up for air after swimming laps. He dangled his legs over the side of the pool. "Something sporty."

I was wearing a two-piece bathing suit—halfway between sporty and a bikini.

"Should I be insulted?" I asked, swimming to the opposite side of the pool and pulling myself up onto the ledge.

"No," Michael replied. "But you are."

He was right, of course. In the dim light of the moon, I wondered how he could even see my face, let alone read an emotion I was trying to hide.

"You like it here." Michael lowered himself into the pool, and for the first time, I registered the fact that his chest was bare. "You like Agent Locke. You like all of her little lessons. And you like the idea of helping out with real cases even more."

I didn't say anything. Clearly, Michael was capable of having this conversation all by himself.

"What? You aren't even going to try to profile me?" Michael flicked water at my knees. "Where's the girl from the diner?" he asked me. "Tit for tat."

"You don't want to be profiled," I told him. "You don't want people to know you." I paused. "You don't want *me* to know you."

He was silent for one second, two, three—and then, "Truth."

"Yeah," I said wryly. "I speak the truth."

"No," Michael replied. "*Truth.* Isn't that what you wanted me to say last night, instead of *dare*?"

"I don't know," I told him, grinning. "I wouldn't trade the memory of your ballet man-dance for anything."

Michael pushed off from the ledge and started treading water. "I also excel at synchronized swimming." I laughed, and he made his way over to my ledge. "I mean it, Cassie. Truth." He paused, two feet away from me. "You ask. I'll tell you. Anything."

I waited for the catch, but there wasn't one.

"Fine," I said, considering my questions carefully. "Why

don't you want to be profiled? What is it you're so afraid that people are going to find out?"

"I got into a fight once," Michael said, sounding oddly at ease. "Right before I came here. Put the other guy in the hospital. I just kept hitting him, over and over again, even once he was down. I don't lose it often, but when I do, it's bad. I take after the old man in that. We Townsends don't do anything halfway." Michael paused. He'd answered my second question, but not my first. "Maybe I don't want to be profiled because *I* don't want to know what you'd see. What little box I fit in. Who I really am."

"There's nothing wrong with you," I said.

He gave me a lazy smile. "That's a matter of some debate."

I'd been planning on asking about his father, but now I couldn't bring myself to ask if the old man had ever *lost it* with him. "Your family's wealthy?"

"As sin," Michael replied. "My past is a long string of boarding schools, excess, and the finest fill-in-the-blank that money can buy."

"Does your family know you're here?"

Michael pushed off the side and started treading water again. I couldn't make out the expression on his face, but I didn't need to see him to know that his trademark smirk held more than a hint of self-loathing. "A better question might be if they care."

Three questions. Three honest answers. Just because he'd offered to show me his scars didn't mean I had to tear them open. "You and Lia?" I asked, changing the subject.

"Yes," Michael replied, catching me off guard, because I hadn't considered it a yes-or-no question. "On again, off again. Never for very long, and it was never a good call—for either of us."

If I didn't want to know the answer, I shouldn't have asked. I stood up and cannonballed back into the pool, sending a small tsunami of water Michael's way. The moment I came back up, he flicked water at my face.

"You know, of course," he said solemnly, "that this means war."

One second, there was a good three feet of space between us, and the next, we were wrestling, each trying to outdunk and outsplash the other, neither of us fully aware of just how close together our bodies were.

I got a mouthful of water. I sputtered. Michael dunked me, and I came up gasping for air—and saw Dean standing on the patio. He was standing perfectly, horribly still.

Michael dunked me again before he realized I'd stopped fighting. He turned around and saw Dean.

"You got a problem, Redding?" Michael asked.

"No," Dean replied. "No problem."

I gave Michael a sharp look and trusted that he'd be able

to read me well enough for it to be effective, even in the dark.

Michael got the message. "Care to join us?" he asked Dean, overly politely.

"No," Dean replied, just as politely. "Thank you." He paused, and the silence swelled around us. "You two have a good night."

As Dean disappeared back into the house, I couldn't help feeling that I'd taken something from him—the place he came to think, the moment we'd shared the night he'd shown me the black lights.

"Truth or dare." Michael's voice cut into my thoughts.

"What?"

"Your turn," Michael told me. "Truth or dare?"

"Truth."

Michael reached out to push my wet hair out of my face. "If Lia had dared you to kiss me, would you have done it?"

"Lia wouldn't have dared me to kiss you."

"But if she had?"

I could feel heat rising in my cheeks. "It was just a game, Michael."

Michael leaned forward and brushed his lips against mine. Then he pulled back and studied my face. Whatever he saw there, he liked.

"Thank you," he said. "That's all I needed to know."

— — —

I didn't sleep much that night. I just kept thinking about Michael and Dean, the subtle barbs that passed between the two of them, the feel of each one's lips. By the time the sun came up the next morning, I wanted to kill someone. Preferably Michael—but Lia was a close second.

"We're out of ice cream," I said murderously.

"True," Lia replied. She'd swapped the silk pajamas for boxer shorts and a ratty T, and there wasn't so much as a hint of remorse on her face.

"I blame you," I said.

"Also true." Lia studied my face. "And unless I'm mistaken, you're not just blaming me for the ice cream. And that makes me terribly curious, Cassie. Care to share?"

It was impossible to keep a secret in this house—let alone two. First Dean, then Michael. I hadn't signed up for this. If Lia hadn't dared me to kiss Dean, Michael never would have kissed me in the pool, and I wouldn't be in this mess, unsure what I felt, what they felt, what I was supposed to do about it.

"No," I said out loud. I was here for one reason and one reason alone. "Forget breakfast," I said, slamming the freezer door shut. "I have work to do."

I turned to leave, but not before I caught sight of Lia twirling her gleaming black ponytail around her index finger, her dark eyes watching me a little too closely for comfort.

CHAPTER 19

I made my way to the library to drown my sorrows in serial killer interviews. Wall-to-wall, ceiling-to-floor bookshelves bulged with carefully organized titles: textbooks, memoirs, biographies, academic journals, and the oddest assortment of fiction I'd ever seen: old-fashioned dime-store mysteries, romance novels, comic books, Dickens, Tolkien, and Poe.

The third shelf from the left was full of blue binders. I picked up the first one and opened it.

FRIEDMAN, THOMAS
OCTOBER 22–28, 1993
FLORIDA STATE PRISON, STARKE, FL

Thomas Friedman. Such a normal-sounding name. Gingerly, I flipped through the transcript: a bare-bones play with a limited cast of characters, no plot, and no resolution. Supervisory Special Agent Cormack Kent was the interviewer. He asked Friedman about his childhood, his parents, his fantasies, the nine women he'd strangled with high-sheen dress hose. Reading Friedman's words—black ink typed onto the page—would have been bad enough, but the worst part was that after a few pages, I could *hear* the way he would have talked about the women he'd killed: excitement, nostalgia, longing—but no remorse.

"You should sit down."

I'd been expecting someone to join me in the library. I hadn't expected that someone to be Lia.

"Dean's not coming," Lia said. "He read those interviews a long time ago."

"Have you read them?" I asked.

"Some," Lia replied. "Mostly, I've *heard* them. Briggs gives me the audio. I play Spot the Lie. It's a real party."

I realized suddenly that most people my age—most people *any* age—wouldn't be able to take reading these interviews. They wouldn't want to, and they certainly wouldn't lose themselves in it, the way I would. The way I already *had*. Friedman's interview was horrible and horrifying—but I couldn't turn off the part of my brain that wanted to *understand*.

"What's the deal with you and Dean?" I asked Lia, forcing myself to think about anything other than the fact that part of me *wanted* to keep reading. Michael might have told me that he and Lia had hooked up—more than once—but Dean was the one who could dial her back a notch just by saying her name.

"I've been in love with him since I was twelve." Lia shrugged, like she hadn't just bared her soul to me. And then I realized, she *hadn't*.

"Oh, God," she said, gasping for air between giggles. "You should see your face. Really, Cassie, I'm not a fan of incest, and Dean is the closest thing to a brother I have. If I tried to kiss him, he might actually hurl on me."

That was comforting. But the fact that it was comforting just sent me right back into the tailspin from that morning: why should I *care* if there was anything between Lia and Dean, when Michael was the one who'd kissed me of his own free will?

"Look, as adorable as watching you angst is," Lia said, "take a bit of friendly advice: there's not a person in this house who isn't really, truly, fundamentally screwed up to the depths of their dark and shadowy souls. Including you. Including Dean. Including Michael."

That sounded more like an insult than advice.

"Dean would want me to tell you to stay away from him," Lia said.

"And Michael?" I asked.

Lia shrugged. "*I* want to tell you to stay away from

Michael." She paused. "I won't, but I want to."

I waited to see if she was finished. She didn't say anything else.

"As far as advice goes, that kind of sucked."

Lia executed an elaborate bow. "I try." Her eyes flitted back to the binder in my hand. "Do me a favor?"

"What kind of favor?"

Lia gestured to the binder. "If you're going to read those," she said, "don't say anything about them to Dean."

For the next four days, Locke and Briggs were away working on their case, and other than avoiding Michael and Dean and weeding the flower beds for Judd, there was nothing for me to do but read. And read. And read. A thousand pages of interviews later, I got sick of being cooped up in the library and decided to take a little field trip. I took a walk through town and ended up plopping down by the Potomac River, enjoying the view and reading interview twenty-seven, binder twelve. The 1990s had given way to the twenty-first century, and SSA Kent had been replaced by a series of other agents—among them, Agent Briggs.

"Enjoying a bit of light reading?"

I looked up to see a man around my dad's age. He had a five-o'clock shadow and a friendly smile on his face.

I shifted so that my arm covered my reading material in case he decided to look. "Something like that."

"You looked pretty absorbed."

Then why did you interrupt me? I wanted to ask. Either he'd sought me out specifically, or he was the kind of person who didn't see the contradiction in interrupting someone's reading to tell her she looked absorbed in the text.

"You live at Judd's place, right?" he said. "He and I go way back."

I relaxed slightly, but still had no intention of getting sucked into a conversation about my reading material— or anything else. "It's nice to meet you," I said in my best waitress voice, hoping he'd sense a false note under the cheerfulness in my voice and leave me to my own devices.

"Enjoying the weather?" he asked me.

"Something like that."

"I can't take you anywhere." Michael appeared on my other side and eased himself onto the ground next to me. "She's too gregarious for her own good," he told the man standing next to us. "Always chatting up complete strangers. Frankly, I think she over-shares. It's embarrassing."

I put the heel of my hand on Michael's shoulder and shoved, but couldn't push down the stab of gratitude I felt that I was no longer suffering through Small Town Talk Time alone.

"Well," the man said. "I didn't mean to interrupt. I just wanted to say hello."

Michael nodded austerely. "How do you do?"

I waited until our visitor was out of earshot before I turned to him. "'How do you do'?" I repeated incredulously.

Michael shrugged. "Sometimes," he said, "when I'm in a social pickle, I like to ask myself, WWJAD?" I raised an eyebrow, and he explained. "What Would Jane Austen Do?"

If Michael read Jane Austen, I was the heir to the British throne.

"What are you doing here?" I asked him.

"Rescuing you," he answered blithely. "What are you doing here?"

I gestured to the binder. "Reading."

"And avoiding me?" he asked.

I repositioned my body and hoped the glare from the sun would compromise his view of my face. "I'm not avoiding anyone. I just wanted to be alone."

Michael brought his hand up to his face to shield it from the sun. "You wanted to be alone," he repeated. "To read."

"That's why I'm here," I said defensively. "That's why we're all here. To learn."

Not to obsess over the fact that I've kissed more boys in the past week than I have in my entire life, I added silently. To my surprise, Michael didn't comment on the emotions I had to be broadcasting. He just reclined next to me and held up some reading material of his own.

"Jane Austen," I said, disbelieving.

Michael gestured toward my binder. "Carry on."

For fifteen or twenty minutes, the two of us read in silence. I finished interview twenty-seven and started in on number twenty-eight.

REDDING, DANIEL
JANUARY 15–18, 2007
VIRGINIA STATE PENITENTIARY, RICHMOND, VA

I almost missed it, would have missed it had the name not been printed over and over again, documenting this particular serial killer's every word.

Redding.

Redding.

Redding.

The interviewer was Agent Briggs. The subject's name was Redding, and he'd been incarcerated in Virginia. I stopped breathing. My mouth went suddenly dry. I flipped through the pages, faster and faster, skimming at warp speed until Daniel Redding asked Briggs a question about his son.

Dean.

ean's father was a serial killer. While I was traveling the country with my mom, Dean had been living twenty yards away from the shack where his father tortured and killed at least a dozen women.

And Dean had never said a word to me: not when we were working our way through Locke's puzzles and bouncing ideas off each other; not when he caught me swimming in the pool that first time; not after we'd kissed. He'd told me that spending time inside the minds of killers would ruin me, but hadn't breathed a word about his past.

Suddenly, everything fell into place. The tone in Lia's voice when she'd said the pictures on the stairwell were there for *Dean's* benefit. The fact that Agent Briggs had gone to Dean for help on a case when he was *twelve*. Michael introducing Dean by telling me that he knew more about the ways that killers thought than just about anyone. Lia asking me, as a favor, not to say anything about these interviews to Dean. *The Bad Seed.*

I stood up and shoved the binder back into my bag. Michael said my name, but I ignored him. I was halfway back to the house before I'd even registered the fact that I was running.

What was I doing?

I didn't have an answer to that question. And yet, I couldn't turn around. I kept going until I reached the house. I climbed the stairs, heading for my room, but Dean was waiting for me at the top, like he'd known today would be the day.

"You've been reading the interviews," he said.

"Yeah," I replied softly. "I have.

"Did you start with Friedman?" Dean asked.

I nodded, waiting for him to name the awful unspoken something that hung in the air between us.

"That's the guy with the panty hose, right? Did you get to the part where he talks about watching his older sister get dressed? Or what about that bit with the neighbor's dog?"

I'd never heard Dean sound like this—so flippant and cruel.

"I don't want to talk about Friedman," I said.

"Right," Dean replied. "You want to talk about my father. Did you read the whole interview? On day three, Briggs bribed him to talk about his childhood. You know what he bribed him with? Pictures of me. And when that didn't work, pictures of *them*. The women he killed."

"Dean—"

"What? Isn't this what you wanted? To talk about it?"

"No," I said. "I want to talk about *you*."

"Me?" Dean couldn't have sounded more incredulous if he'd tried. "What else is there to say?"

What *was* there to say?

"I don't care." My breath was still ragged from running. I was saying this wrong. "Your father—it doesn't change who you are."

"*What* I am," he corrected. "And yes, it does. Why don't you go ask Sloane what the statistics say about psychopathy and heredity? And then why don't you ask her what they say about growing up in an environment where it's the only thing you know."

"I don't care about the statistics," I said. "We're partners. We work together. You knew I was going to find out. You could have told me."

"We're not partners."

The words hurt me—and he meant for them to.

"We won't ever be partners," Dean said, his voice razor sharp and unrepentant. "And do you want to know why? Because as good as you are at getting inside normal people's heads, I don't even have to *work* to get inside a killer's. Doesn't that bother you? Didn't you ever notice how easy it was for me to be the monster when we were 'working' together?"

I'd noticed—but I'd attributed it to the fact that Dean had more experience at profiling killers. I hadn't realized that that experience was firsthand.

"Did you know about your father?" I regretted the question the moment I asked it, but Dean didn't bat an eye.

"No," he said. "Not at first, but I should have."

Not at *first*?

"I told you, Cassie. By the time Briggs started coming by with questions on cases, there was nothing left to ruin."

"That's not true, Dean."

"My father was in prison. I was in foster care, and even back then, I knew that I wasn't like the other kids. The way my mind worked, the things that *made sense* to me . . ." He turned his back on me. "I think you should go."

"Go? Go where?"

"I. Don't. Care." He let out a shuddery breath. "Just leave me alone."

"I don't want to leave you alone." And there it was, something I hadn't even let myself *think* since Truth or Dare.

"How exactly was I supposed to tell you?" Dean asked, still facing away from me. "'Hey, guess what? Your mom was murdered, and my dad is a killer.'"

"This isn't about my mom."

"What do you want me to say, Cassie?" Dean finally

turned back around to face me. "Just tell me, and I'll say it."

"I just want you to talk to me."

Dean's fingers curled into fists at his sides. I could barely see his eyes behind the hair that fell in his face. "I don't want to talk to you," he said. "You're better off with Michael."

"Dean—"

A hand grabbed my shoulder and spun me around. Hard.

"He said he didn't want to talk to you, Cassie." Lia's face was a mask of calm. Her tone was anything but. "Don't turn back to look at him. Don't say another word to him. Just go. And one more thing?" She leaned forward to whisper in my ear. "Remind me never to ask you for a favor again."

CHAPTER 21

I walked slowly back down the stairs, trying to figure out what had just happened. What was I thinking, confronting Dean? He was allowed to have secrets. He was allowed to be angry that Locke had assigned me to read those interviews, knowing that one of them was his father's. I shouldn't have gone up there. I should have left him alone.

"Lia or Dean?"

I looked up and saw Michael standing near the front door.

"What?"

"The look on your face," he replied. "Lia or Dean?"

I shrugged. "Both?"

Michael nodded, as if my answer were a foregone conclusion. "You okay?"

"You're the emotion reader," I said. "You tell me."

He took that as an invitation to come closer. He stopped

a foot or two away and studied my face. "You're confused. Madder at yourself than you are at either of them. Lonely. Angry. Stupid."

"Stupid?" I sputtered.

"Hey, I just call it like I see it." Michael was apparently in the mood to be blunt. "You feel stupid. Doesn't mean you are."

"Why didn't you tell me?" I sat down on the bottom step, and after a few seconds, Michael sat down beside me, stretching his legs out on the hardwood floor. "Why make thinly veiled comments about *The Bad Seed* instead of just telling me the truth?"

"I thought about telling you." Michael leaned back on his elbows, his casual posture contradicting the tension unmistakable in his voice. "Every time I saw the two of you hunched over one of Locke's little puzzles, I thought about telling you. But what would you have said if I did?"

I tried to imagine hearing about Dean's father from Michael, who could barely manage a civil word where Dean was concerned.

"Exactly." Michael reached forward to tap the edge of my lips, like that was the precise spot that had tipped him off to what was going on inside my mind. "You wouldn't have thanked me for telling you. You would have hated me for it."

I swatted Michael's hand away from my face. "I wouldn't have hated you."

Michael gestured in the general direction of my forehead, but refrained from actually touching my face this time. "Your mouth says one thing, but your eyebrows say another." He paused, and his own mouth twisted into a lazy grin. "You might not realize this, Colorado, but you can be a little sanctimonious."

This time, I didn't bother letting my face do the talking for me. I slugged him in the shoulder—hard.

"Fine." Michael held his palms up in surrender. "You're not sanctimonious. You're honorable." He paused and trained his eyes straight ahead. "Maybe I didn't want to advertise the fact that I'm not."

For a split second, Michael let those words—that confession—hang in the air.

"Besides," he continued, "if I'd told you that between Redding and myself I was the safe option, I would have lost all of that carefully built-up bad-boy cred."

From self-loathing to sardonic in under two seconds.

"Trust me," I said lightly, "you don't have any cred."

"Oh, really?" Michael said. When I nodded, he stood up and took my hand. "Let's fix that, then, shall we?"

A wiser person would have said no. I took a deep breath. "What did you have in mind?"

Blowing stuff up was surprisingly therapeutic.

"Clear!" Michael yelled. The two of us scuttled backward.

A second later, a string of fireworks went off, scorching the floor of a fake foyer.

"Somehow, I don't think this is what Agent Briggs had in mind when he built this basement," I said.

Michael adopted an austere look. "Simulation is one of our most powerful tools," he said, doing a passable imitation of Agent Briggs. "How else are we to visualize the work of the infamous Boom-Boom Bandit?"

"Boom-Boom Bandit?" I repeated.

He grinned. "Too much?"

I held my index finger up an inch from my thumb. "Just a little."

Behind us, the door to the basement opened and slammed shut. I half expected it to be Judd, asking what precisely we thought we were doing down here, but Michael had assured me the basement was soundproof.

"I didn't know anyone was down here." Sloane looked at the two of us suspiciously. "Why *are* you down here?"

Michael and I looked at each other. I opened my mouth to answer, but Sloane's eyes widened as she took in the evidence.

"Fireworks?" she said, folding her arms over her middle. "In the foyer?"

Michael shrugged. "Cassie needed a distraction, and I needed to give Briggs a few more gray hairs."

Sloane eyed him mutinously. Considering the amount of

time she spent down here, I could see why she might take any misuse of the crime sets seriously.

"Sorry," I said.

"You should be," she replied sternly. "You're doing it all wrong."

What followed was a ten-minute lecture on pyrodynamics. And several more explosions.

"Well," Michael said, surveying our work. "That'll teach Briggs and Locke to leave us to our own devices for too long."

I shoved my hair out of my face with the heel of my hand. "They're working a case," I said, remembering the look on Locke's face—and the details I'd managed to glean about what she and Briggs were up to. "I think that's a little bit of a higher priority than training us is."

"Sloane," Michael said suddenly, drawing out her name and narrowing his eyes.

"Nothing," Sloane replied quickly.

"Nothing what?" I asked. Clearly, I was missing something here.

"When I said Locke's name, Sloane looked down and to the side and her eyebrows pulled up in the center." Michael paused, and when he spoke again, his voice was softer. "What did you take, Sloane?"

Sloane made a careful study of her fingernails. "Agent Locke doesn't like me."

I thought back to the last time I had seen Sloane and

Locke together. Sloane had come into the kitchen and rattled off some statistics about serial killers. Locke hadn't had a chance to reply when Briggs came into the room with an update on their case. In fact, I wasn't sure I'd ever seen Locke say anything to Sloane, though she traded barbs easily enough with Michael and Lia.

"There was a USB drive," Sloane admitted finally, "in Agent Locke's briefcase."

Michael's eyes lit up. "Am I to infer that you have it now?"

Sloane shrugged. "That's a distinct possibility."

"You took a USB drive out of Locke's briefcase?" I processed that bit of information. When Lia had helped herself to the contents of my closet, she'd said that Sloane was the kleptomaniac in the house. I'd assumed she was joking.

Apparently not.

"Let's concentrate on the important thing here," Michael said. "What information do you lovely ladies think Locke would be carrying on her person while working a case?"

I glanced at Sloane, then back at Michael. "You think it has something to do with their current case?" I couldn't keep the surge of interest out of my tone.

"That is also a distinct possibility." Sloane was sounding distinctly more chipper.

Michael threw an arm over her shoulder. "Have I ever told you that you're my favorite?" he asked her. Then he cast a wicked glance at me. "Still in need of distraction?"

CHAPTER 22

"This encryption is pathetic," Sloane said. "It's like they *want* me to hack their files."

She was sitting cross-legged on the end of her bed, her laptop balanced on her knees. Her fingers flew across the keys as she worked on breaking through the protection on the pilfered USB drive. A stray piece of blond hair drifted into her face, but she didn't seem to notice. "Done!"

Sloane turned the laptop around so the two of us could see it. "Seven files," she said. The smile fell from her face. "Seven victims."

Locke's lecture on victimology came flooding back to me. Was that why my mentor had been carrying around a digital copy of these files? Had she been attempting to get inside the victims' heads?

"What if this is important?" I asked, unable to push back

a stab of guilt. "What if Locke and Briggs need this information for their case?" I'd come to the program to help, not to get in the way of the FBI's efforts.

"Cassie," Michael said, taking a seat against the foot of the bed and stretching his legs out in front of him. "Is Briggs the type to keep backups?"

Agent Briggs was the type to keep backups of his backups. He and Locke had been gone for three days. If they'd needed this drive, they would have come back for it.

"Should I print out the files?" Sloane asked.

Michael looked at me and raised an eyebrow. "Your call, Colorado."

I should have said no. I should have told Sloane that the case Locke and Briggs were working on was none of our business, but I'd come here to help, and Locke *had* said that she and Briggs had hit a brick wall.

"Print it."

A second later, the printer on Sloane's desk started spitting out pages. After fifty or so sheets, it stopped. Michael leaned over and grabbed the pages. He separated them by case and helped himself to three case files before handing the others to Sloane and me. All seven were homicides. Four in DC in the past two weeks, and another three cases, all within the past year, from other jurisdictions.

"First DC victim disappeared from the street she was working ten days ago and showed up the next morning with her face half carved off." Michael looked up from leafing through the file.

"This one's dated three days later," I said. "Facial mutilation, numerous superficial cuts to the rest of the body—she died of blood loss."

"This would take time," Sloane said, her face pale. "Hours, not minutes, and according to the autopsy reports, the tissue damage is—*severe*."

"He's playing with them." Michael finished with his second file and started in on the third. "He takes them. He cuts them. He watches them suffer. And then he cuts off their faces."

"Don't say *he*," I corrected absentmindedly. "Say *I* or *you*."

Michael and Sloane both stared at me, and I realized the obvious: their lessons were very different from mine.

"I mean, say *UNSUB*," I told them. "Unknown Subject."

"I can think of some better names for this guy," Michael murmured, looking through the last case file in his hands. "Who has the file for the last victim?"

"I do." Sloane's voice was quiet, and suddenly, she looked very young. "She was a palm reader in Dupont Circle." For a second, I thought Sloane might actually put the file down, but then her features went suddenly calm. "A person is ten times more likely to become a professional athlete than to make a living reading palms," she said, taking refuge in the numbers.

Most killers have a type, I thought, falling back on my own lessons. "Do any of the other victims have ties to the psychic community, astrology, or the occult?"

Michael turned back to the two reports in his hand. "Lady of the Evening," he said, "another Lady of the Evening, and a telemarketer . . . who worked at a psychic hotline."

I glanced down at the two files in my hand. "I've got a nineteen-year-old runaway and a medium working out of Los Angeles."

"Two different kinds of victims," Michael observed. "Prostitutes, drifters, and runaways in column A. People with a tie to the occult in column B."

I fished Before photos of the victims out of my files and gestured for the others to do the same.

You pick them for a reason, I thought, looking at the women one by one. *You cut their faces, slice your knife down through skin and tissue, until you hit the bone. This is personal.*

"They're all young," I said, studying them and searching for commonalities. "Between eighteen and thirty-five."

"Those three have red hair." Michael separated out the victims with no ties to the psychic community.

"The palm reader had red hair, too," Sloane interjected.

I was staring directly at the palm reader's Before picture. "The palm reader was a blonde."

"No," Sloane said slowly. "She was a *natural* blonde. But when they found her, she looked like this."

Sloane slid a second, gruesome picture toward us. True to Sloane's words, the corpse's hair was a deep, unmistakable red.

A recent dye job, I thought. *So did she dye her hair . . . or did you?*

"Two classes of victims," Michael said again, lining the redheads up in one column and the psychics in another, with the palm reader from Dupont Circle between the two. "You think we're looking for two different killers?"

"No," I said. "We're only looking for one killer."

My companions could make observations. Sloane could generate relevant statistics. If there'd been witness testimony, Michael could have told us who was exhibiting signs of guilt. But here, now, looking at the pictures, this was my domain. I would have had to backtrack to explain how I knew, to *figure out* how I knew—but I was certain. The pictures, what had been done to these women, it was the same. Not just the details, but the anger, the urges . . .

All of these women had been killed by the same person.

You're escalating, I thought. *Something happened, and now you need more, faster.*

I stared at the photos, my mind whirring, picking up each detail of the pictures, the files, until only three things stood out.

Knife.

Redhead.

Psychic.

That was the moment that the ground disappeared from underneath me. I lost the ability to blink. My eyes got very dry. My throat was worse. My vision blurred, and all of the photographs got very fuzzy except for one.

The nineteen-year-old runaway.

The hair, the facial structure, the freckles. Through blurred vision, she looked like . . .

Knife.

Redhead.

Psychic.

"Cassie?" Michael took my hands in his. "You're freezing."

"The UNSUB is killing redheads," I said, "and he's killing psychics."

"That's not a pattern," Sloane said peevishly. "That's two patterns."

"No," I said, "it's not. I think . . ."

Knife. Redhead. Psychic.

I couldn't say the words. "My mother . . ." I took a short breath and brutally expelled it. "I don't know what my mother's body looked like," I said finally, "but I do know that she was attacked with a knife."

Michael and Sloane stared at me. I got up and walked over to my dresser. I opened the top drawer and found what I was looking for.

A picture.

Don't look at it, I thought.

Directing my gaze at anything but the picture in my hand, I stooped and tapped my fingers on the palm reader's photograph. "I don't think she dyed her hair red," I said. "I think the killer did."

You kill psychics. You kill redheads. But one or the other isn't enough anymore. It's never enough.

Glancing up at Michael and Sloane, I laid my mother's picture down between the two columns.

Sloane studied it. "She looks like the other victims," she said, nodding to the column of redheads.

"No," I said. "They look like her."

These women had all been killed in the past nine months. My mother had been missing for five years.

"Cassie, who is that?" Michael had to have known the answer to that question, but he asked it anyway.

"That's my mother." I still couldn't let myself look at the picture. "She was attacked with a knife. Her body was never found." I paused, just for a second. "My mother made her living by convincing people she was psychic."

Michael looked at me—and *into* me. "Are you saying what I think you're saying?"

I was saying that Briggs and Locke were tracking an UNSUB who killed women with red hair and people who claimed to be psychic. It could have been a coincidence. I should have assumed it was a coincidence.

But I didn't.

"I'm saying this killer has a very specific type: people who resemble my mother."

YOU

Last night, you woke up in a cold sweat, and the only voice in your head was your father's. The dream seemed real. It always seems real. You could feel the sticky sheets, smell the urine, hear the whistle of His hand tearing through the air. You woke up shaking, and then you realized—

The bed was wet.

No, *you thought.* No. No. No.

But there wasn't anyone there to punish you. Your father's dead, and you're not.

You're the one who does the punishing now.

But it's never enough. The neighbor's dog. The whores. Even the palm reader wasn't enough. You open the bathroom cabinet. One by one, you run your hands over each of the tubes of lipstick, remember each of the girls.

It's calming.

Soothing.

Exciting.

You stop when you get to the oldest tube. The first. You know what you want. What you need. You've always known.

All that's left to do now is take it.

CHAPTER 23

When I'd found out about Dean's dad, I'd taken off running, but now that my mom's photograph was staring up at me from a sea of murder victims, all I could do was sit there.

"Maybe this was a bad idea." Coming from Michael, those words sounded completely alien.

"No," I said. "You wanted to distract me. I'm distracted."

"The likelihood that this UNSUB is the one who attacked your mother is extremely low." Sloane spoke hesitantly, like she thought one more word—or one more statistic—might set me off. "This killer abducts his victims and kills them at a separate location, leaving little to no physical evidence at the site of abduction. There's some indication that at least two of the victims may have been drugged. The women have relatively few defensive wounds, indicating that they're likely restrained before the knife comes into play."

Sloane was talking about this killer's MO. With her gift, that was as far as she could go. She couldn't see underneath it, couldn't imagine how a killer might have refined his technique over the span of five years.

"When does Agent Briggs get back?" I asked.

"He's never going to let you work on this," Michael told me.

"Is that your way of telling me that you don't want him to know we hacked a stolen jump drive?" I shot back.

Michael snorted. "Personally, I wouldn't mind taking out an ad in the paper or hiring a skywriter to announce that he and Locke were outsmarted by three bored teenagers."

I could think of a lot of words to describe my life right now; *boring* wasn't one of them.

"Briggs is nothing if not predictable, Cassie. His job is proving that we can solve cold cases, not dragging us along on active ones. He's probably lucky his bosses didn't fire him when they figured out what he was doing with Dean. Even if this case does have something to do with your mother's, he'll never let you work on it."

I turned to Sloane for a second opinion.

"Two hours and fifty-six minutes," she said. "Briggs was due back in town today, but he'll need to settle things at the office and grab a change of clothes and a shower before coming in."

That meant I had two hours and fifty-six minutes to

decide how to broach this case to Agent Briggs—or better yet, Agent Locke.

The good thing about being in cahoots with an emotion reader was that Michael could tell that I wanted to be left alone, and he obliged. Better yet, he took Sloane—and the files—with him.

If he hadn't, I probably would still have been sitting there, staring at the crime-scene photos and wondering if my mom had died without a face. Instead, I was lying on my bed, staring at the door and trying to think of something—*anything*—I could offer the FBI to make them want me on this case.

Two hours and forty-two minutes later, someone knocked on my door. I thought it might be Agent Briggs, back fourteen minutes earlier than Sloane had predicted.

But it wasn't.

"Dean?"

He hadn't ever sought me out *before* he'd told me that we weren't partners, weren't friends, weren't anything. I couldn't imagine why he'd come looking for me voluntarily now.

"Can I come in?"

There was something about the way he was standing there that told me he was expecting me to say no. Maybe I should have. Instead, I nodded, not trusting my voice.

He came in and shut the door behind him. "Lia eavesdrops," he explained, gesturing toward the closed door.

I shrugged and waited for him to say something he wouldn't want overheard.

"I'm sorry." He managed two words, paused, and then pushed out two more. "About before."

"You have nothing to be sorry about." There was no law saying he had to trust me. Outside of Locke's lessons, we'd barely spent any time together. He hadn't *chosen* to kiss me.

"Lia told me about the files you and Michael and Sloane found."

The sudden change of subject took me by surprise. "How does Lia even know about that?"

Dean shrugged. "She eavesdrops."

And since I wasn't exactly Lia's favorite person right now, she had no reason whatsoever to keep her mouth closed about whatever it was that she'd overheard.

"So, what?" I asked Dean. "We're even now? I found out about your dad and Lia told you that I think the UNSUB Briggs and Locke are after might be the one who killed my mom and now everything's okay?"

Dean sat down on Sloane's bed and faced me. "Nothing's okay."

Why was it that I'd managed to hold on to my cool with Michael and Sloane, but now that Dean was here, I could feel myself starting to slip?

"Sloane said that she thinks it's highly unlikely that this killer is the same one who took my mother," I said, looking down at my lap and trying not to cry. "It's been five years. The MO is different. I don't even know if the signature is the same, because they never found my mother's body."

Dean leaned forward and angled his head up at mine. "Some killers go for years without being caught, and their MOs change as time goes on. They learn. They evolve. They need *more*."

Dean was telling me that I could be right, that the time frame didn't preclude this being the same UNSUB, but I knew from his tone of voice that he wasn't just talking about *this* UNSUB.

"How long was it before they caught him?" I asked softly. I didn't specify who *him* was. I didn't have to.

Dean met my gaze and held it. "Years."

I wondered if that one word was more than he'd told anyone else about his father.

I thought that maybe it was.

"My mother. I was the one who found . . ." I couldn't say *her body* because there hadn't been one. I swallowed hard, but I kept going, because it was important, somehow, to put it into words, to tell him.

"I'd gone to check out the crowd, eavesdrop, see if there was anything I could pick up on that might help my mom during the show. I was gone ten minutes, maybe fifteen, and when I got back, she was gone. The entire room had been tossed. The police say she fought. I *know* she fought—but there was so much blood. I don't know how many times he stabbed her, but when I got back to the room, I could smell it. The door was partway open. The light was off. I stepped into the room and I felt something wet underneath my feet. I said her name, I think. And then I reached for the light switch. I got the wall instead, and there was blood on the wall. It was on my hands, Dean, and then I turned on the light, and it was everywhere."

Dean didn't say anything, but he was there, so close that I could feel the heat of his body next to mine. He was listening, and I couldn't shake the feeling that he understood.

"I'm sorry," I said. "I don't usually talk about this, and I don't let it do this to me, but I remember thinking that whoever hurt my mother hated her. He knew her, and he hated her, Dean. It was there, in the room, in the spatter, in the way she'd fought—it wasn't random. *He knew her,* and how could I explain that to anyone? Who would have believed me? I was just some stupid kid, but now Briggs and Locke have this case, and their UNSUB is killing people who look like my mother and people who hold a similar job, and he's doing it with a knife. And even though the victims are scattered geographically, even though none of them knew each other, it's personal." I paused. "I don't think he's killing them. I think he's killing *her* again. And I'm not just some stupid kid anymore. I'm a profiler. A Natural. But even so—who's going to believe me?"

Dean put a hand on my neck, the way he had the first time I'd crawled into a killer's mind. "Nobody is going to believe you," he said. "You're too close to it." He ran his thumb up and down the side of my neck. "But Briggs will believe me."

Dean was the only person in this house who shared my ability. Michael and Sloane might have been skeptical about my theory, but Dean had instincts like mine. He'd know if I was crazy, or if there was something to this. "You'll look at the case?" I asked him.

He nodded and dropped his hand from my neck, like he'd only just realized he was touching me.

I stood. "I'll be right back," I said. "I'm going to get the file."

CHAPTER 24

"Michael, can I have the—" I burst into the kitchen, only to find that Michael and Sloane weren't the only ones there. Judd was cooking, and Agent Briggs was standing with his back to me, a thin black briefcase by his feet.

"—the bacon," I finished hastily.

Agent Briggs turned to face me. "And why does Michael have your bacon?" he asked.

As if this whole situation wasn't awkward enough, Lia chose that moment to come sauntering into the room. "Yes, Cassie," she said with a wicked grin, "tell us why Michael *has your bacon.*"

The way she said the phrase left very little question that she was using it as a euphemism.

"Lia," Judd said, waving a spatula in her general direction, "that's enough." Then he turned to me. "Grub will be ready soon. I expect you can hold out until then?"

"Yes," I said. "No bacon needed."

From behind Briggs's back, Michael pantomimed smacking his palm into his forehead. Apparently, my attempts at subterfuge left something to be desired. I tried to make a quick exit, but Agent Briggs stopped me in my tracks.

"Cassie. A word."

I glanced at Michael, wondering what—if anything—Briggs knew about what Michael, Sloane, and I had been up to.

"Ambidextrous," Sloane said suddenly.

"This should be good," Lia murmured.

Sloane cleared her throat. "Agent Briggs asked for a word. *Ambidextrous* is a good one. Less than point-five percent of the words in the English language contain all five vowels."

I was grateful for the distraction, but unfortunately, Briggs didn't bite. "Cassie?"

"Sure." I nodded and followed him out of the room. I wasn't sure where we were heading at first, but after we passed the library, I realized we were going to the only room on the ground floor I hadn't been in yet—Briggs's study.

He opened the door and gestured for me to enter. I walked into the room, taking in my surroundings. The room was full of animals, lifeless and frozen in place.

Hunting trophies.

There was a grizzly bear, reared up on its back legs,

its mouth caught in a silent roar. On the other side of the room, a lifelike panther crouched, canines gleaming, while a mountain lion seemed to be on the prowl.

The most disturbing thing about this entire room—maybe this entire situation—was that I hadn't pegged Agent Briggs for a hunter.

"They're predators. Reminders of what my team deals with every time we go out in the world."

There was something about the way Agent Briggs said those words that made me realize, beyond a shadow of a doubt, that he knew what Michael, Sloane, and I had been up to in his absence. He knew that *we* knew the exact details of the case that he and Agent Locke were working now.

"How did you find out?" I asked.

"Judd told me." Briggs crossed the room and sat on the edge of the desk. He gestured for me to take a seat in a chair in front of him. "You know, Judd might fade into the background around here, but there's not much that goes on in this house that he doesn't know. Information gathering has always been a specialty of his."

Keeping his eyes fixed on me, Briggs opened his briefcase and took out a file: all of the papers we'd printed out earlier. "I confiscated this from Michael. And this," he added, holding up the USB drive, "from Sloane. Her laptop will be making a trip to our tech lab to ensure that all traces of data have been wiped from the hard drive."

I hadn't even had a chance to tell Agent Briggs my suspicions, and he was already shutting me down—and shutting me out.

Briggs ran one hand roughly over his chin, and I realized that he hadn't shaved in at least a day.

"The case isn't going well." I paused. "Is it?"

"I need you to listen to what I'm saying, Cassandra."

That was only the second time he'd called me by my full name since I'd told him I preferred Cassie.

"I was up front with you about what this program is and what it is not. The FBI isn't about to authorize teenagers to dive into the middle of active cases."

His choice of words was more revealing than he knew. The *FBI* had qualms about throwing teenagers into the thick of things. Briggs—personally—did not.

"So what you're saying is that using the twelve-year-old son of a serial killer as your own personal encyclopedia of murderous minds was fine, but now that the program is official, we can't even look at the files?"

"What I'm saying," Briggs countered, "is that this UNSUB is dangerous. He's local. And I have no intention of involving any of you."

"Even if this case has something to do with my mother's?"

Briggs paused. "You're jumping to conclusions." He didn't ask me why I thought this case had something to do with my mother's. Now that I'd brought up the idea, he didn't have to. "The occupations. The red hair. The knife. It isn't enough."

"The UNSUB dyed the latest victim's hair red." I didn't bother asking if I was right about that, knowing in my gut that I was. "That's above and beyond victim selection. It's not just an MO anymore. It's part of the UNSUB's signature."

Briggs crossed his arms over his chest. "I'm not talking with you about this."

And yet, he didn't leave the room—and he didn't stop listening.

"Did the UNSUB dye her hair before or after he killed her?"

Briggs didn't say a word. He was playing this by the book—but he didn't tell me to stop talking, either.

"Dyeing the victim's hair before the kill could be an attempt to create a more ideal target, one who claims to be psychic *and* has red hair. But dyeing her hair afterward . . ." I paused, just long enough to see that Briggs was listening, really listening, to every word. "Dyeing her hair after she's already dead is a message."

"And what message is that?" Agent Briggs asked sharply, like he was dismissing my words out of hand, when both of us knew that he was not.

"A message for you: hair color matters. The UNSUB

wants you to know that there's a connection between the cases. He doesn't trust you to come to that conclusion on your own, so he's helping you get there."

Briggs was silent for three or four loaded seconds.

"We can't do this, Cassie. I understand your interest in the case. I understand your wanting to help, but whatever you think you're doing, it ends now."

I started to object and he held up a hand, silencing me.

"I'll tell Locke to let you start working on cold cases. You're obviously ready. But if you so much as sniff in the direction of *this* case again, there will be consequences, and I can guarantee that you will find them unpleasant." He leaned forward, his posture unconsciously mimicking the roaring bear's. "Have I made myself clear?"

I didn't respond. If he was looking for a promise that I'd stay out of this, he was going to be disappointed.

"I already have a Natural profiler in this program." Briggs looked me straight in the eye, his lips set in a thin, forbidding line. "I'd prefer to have two, but not at the risk of my job."

There it was: the ultimate threat. If I pushed this, Briggs could send me home. Back to Nonna and the aunts and the uncles and the constant awareness that I would never be like them, like *anyone* outside of these walls.

"You've made yourself clear," I said.

Briggs closed his briefcase. "Give it a couple of years, Cassie. They won't keep you out of the field forever."

He waited for my reply, but I said nothing. He stood up and walked to the door.

"If he's dyeing their hair, the rules are changing," I called after him, not bothering to turn around to see if he'd stopped to listen or not. "And that means that before things get better, they're going to get a whole lot worse."

YOU

You can't remember the last time you felt this way. All of the others—all of them—were imitations. A copy of a copy of the thing you wanted most. But now—now you're close.

A smile on your face, you pick up the scissors. The girl on the floor screams, the duct tape stretching tight across her face, but you ignore her. She's not the real prize here, just a means to an end.

You grab her by the hair and jerk her head back. She struggles, and you tighten your grip and slam her head into the wall.

"Be still," you whisper. You let her hair fall back down and then lift a single lock of it up.

You raise the scissors. You cut the hair.

And then you cut her.

CHAPTER 25

I went to bed early. So much had happened in the past twenty-four hours that my body physically *hurt*. I didn't want to be awake anymore. That plan worked for a few hours, but just after midnight, I awoke to the sound of footsteps outside of my door and the dulcet melody of Sloane snoring next to me.

For a second, I thought I'd imagined the footsteps, but then I saw the hint of a shadow underneath the door.

There's someone out there.

Whoever it was just stood there. I crept toward the door, my hair stuck to my forehead with sweat and my heartbeat thudding in my ears.

I opened the door.

"Not going for a swim tonight?"

It took a second for Michael's features to come together in the darkness, but I recognized his voice immediately.

"I don't feel like swimming." I lowered my voice, but not as much as I would have if my roommate's nasal passages hadn't been threatening to deafen me within the year.

"I got you something." Michael took a step forward, until his face was mere inches from mine. Slowly, he held up an inch-thick file.

I looked at him, then at the file, then back at him.

"You didn't," I said.

"Oh yes," he replied. "I did."

"How?" Already, my fingers were itching to snatch the file from his hand.

"Briggs took Sloane's computer. He didn't take mine."

I thought about Briggs's warning, his threat to send me home. And then, slowly, I closed my fingers around the file. "You copied the files onto your laptop."

Michael smiled. "You're welcome."

I tucked the file under my mattress. Maybe there was another clue in there. Maybe there wasn't. First chance I got, I was showing it to Dean. Unfortunately, when I went to find him the next morning, he wasn't alone.

"Miss me?" Agent Locke didn't wait for me to answer her question. "Sit."

I sat. So did Dean.

"Here." Agent Locke held out a thick legal file, the accordion bottom stretched to capacity and then some.

"What's this?" I asked.

"Briggs thinks you're ready to take the next step, Cassie." Locke paused. "Is he right?"

"A cold case?" The file was faded—and much, much heavier than the one tucked under my mattress.

"A string of unsolved murders from the nineties," Locke told us. "Home invasion; one bullet to the head, execution-style. The rest of the file contains all of the similar unsolved homicides that have taken place in that area since."

Dean groaned. "No wonder the file's so thick," he muttered. "A third of all drug-related hits probably look just like this."

"Then I guess it should keep the two of you busy." Locke gave me a look that I took to mean Briggs had told her about our little discussion.

"I'll check in later in the week. You two have a lot of reading to do, and I have a case to solve."

She left the two of us alone. I opened my mouth to say something about the case file jammed under my mattress, but then I closed it again. Lia eavesdropped—and apparently, so did Judd.

"How would you feel about working on our cold case in the basement?" I asked. The *soundproof* basement. It took Dean a moment to catch on, but then he led the way down the stairs, closing the door firmly behind us. We walked the length of the basement, three-walled rooms lining either side, like theater sets in want of a play.

Once I was sure we were alone, I started talking. "When I went to get the file yesterday, Briggs busted me. By the time I got back to my room, you were gone."

"Lia may have mentioned that Briggs busted you," Dean said. "You okay?"

"I told him my theory. I asked to work on the case. He said no."

"You going to work on it anyway?" Dean paused in front of one of the outdoor sets: a partial park. I sat down on a park bench, and he leaned back against the bench's arm.

"I have a copy of the file," I said. "Will you look at it?"

He nodded. Five minutes later, he was elbow-deep in the case—and I had Locke's cold case in my hands, ready to cover in case anyone came down to check on us.

"Sometimes victims are just substitutes," Dean said after he'd read through the entire file. "I'm married, but I'd never get away with killing my own wife, so I kill hookers and pretend that they're her. My kid died, and now every time I see a kid in a baseball cap, I have to make him mine."

Dean had always used the word *I* to climb into killers' heads, but now that I knew his background, hearing that word come out of his mouth gave me chills.

"Maybe the first time I killed someone, it wasn't planned, but now the only time I ever really feel alive is when I'm feeling the life go out of someone else, someone like *her.*"

"You see it, too, don't you?" I asked.

He nodded. "I'd bet money that this person is either reliving their first kill or fantasizing about a person they want to kill but can't."

"And if I told you there was a red-haired psychic attacked with a knife five years ago, and they never found the body?"

Dean paused. "Then I'd want to know everything there was to know about that case," he said.

So did I.

YOU

The box is black. The tissue is white. And the present—the present is red. You lay it gingerly in the tissue. You put the lid on the box. You wash the scissors and use them to cut a long, black ribbon—silk.

Special.

Just like The Girl is.

No, you think, picking up the present and stroking your gloved thumb along its edge. You don't have to call her The Girl. Not anymore.

You've seen her. You've watched her. You're sure. No more imitations. No more copies. It's time she got to know you, the way you knew her mother.

You put the card on top of the package. You scrawl her name on the outside, each letter a labor of love.

C-A-S-S-I-E.

PART THREE:
HUNTING

Wanting to know more about my mother's case and determining the best way to gain access to her file were two very different things. Twenty-four hours after Dean had confirmed my impression of our UNSUB, I was still empty-handed.

"Well, well, well . . ."

I heard Lia's voice, but refused to turn around and watch her make an entrance. Instead, I focused on the grain of the kitchen table and the sandwich on my plate.

"Somebody got a package in the mail," Lia singsonged. "I took the liberty of opening it for you, and voilà. A box within a box." She sat down next to me and placed a rectangular gift box in front of her on the table. "A secret admirer, perhaps?" There was an envelope on top of the box, and Lia picked it up and dangled the card in front of me.

My name was written on the envelope, the letters evenly spaced with just a hint of curl to them, like the person who'd written them was torn between writing in cursive and writing in print.

"You really are *incredibly* popular, aren't you?" Lia said. "It defies all logic. I assumed you were just the new shiny. In a program with so few students, it would be weirder if the new girl *didn't* draw attention from the opposite sex. But neither Michael nor Dean would have a reason to mail you a package, so I can only infer that your, shall we say, *appeal* isn't limited to people who live here."

I tuned Lia out and looked at the box. It was matte black with a perfectly fitted lid. A black ribbon had been wrapped around the box twice, forming a cross shape on the front. In the center of the cross, the ribbon curled into a bow.

"Did I hear my name?" Michael sauntered over to join us. "Don't you just hate it when you walk into the room and everyone's talking about you?" His eyes landed on the gift, and the smile on his face turned plastic and sharp.

"Somebody's not fond of competition," Lia said.

"And somebody is a lot more vulnerable than she lets on," Michael replied without missing a beat. "Your point?"

That shut Lia up—temporarily. I looked back down at the box and ran my finger along the edge of the ribbon.

Silk.

"You didn't send this?" I asked Michael, my voice catching in my throat.

"No," Michael replied with a roll of his eyes. "I really didn't."

There wasn't a person in my family who would have sent me a package wrapped up in silk, and I couldn't think of anyone else who would want to send me a care package.

Michael hadn't sent it.

Dean wasn't the gift-giving type.

I turned to Lia. "You sent this."

"Not true." She stared at me for a second, then made a grab for the card.

"Don't—" I started to say. My words fell on deaf ears. She plucked a plain white note card from the envelope and cleared her throat.

"*From me, to you.*" Lia arched an eyebrow and tossed the card back on the table. "How romantic."

A chill crawled up my spine. My breath felt hot in my lungs, but my hands were freezing cold. The package, the ribbon, the bow tied just so . . .

Something isn't right.

"Cassie?" Michael must have seen it on my face. He leaned toward me. I glanced at Lia, but for once, she had nothing to say. Slowly, I brought my hand up to the ribbon. I pulled, and it fell away into a graceful black heap on the table.

Now that I'd started, I couldn't stop. I hooked my fingers around the lid of the box. I pulled it off and set it gingerly to the side. White tissue paper, meticulously folded, lay inside.

"What is it?"

I ignored Lia's question. I reached into the box. I unwrapped the tissue paper.

And then I screamed.

Nestled in the tissue paper was a lock of red hair.

CHAPTER 27

It took Agent Briggs an hour to get to our house. It took him five seconds to get from the front door to the kitchen—and the box.

"Still think I'm jumping to conclusions when I say this case is related to my mother's?" I asked him, my voice shaky. He ignored me and barked out commands to the team of agents he'd brought with him.

"Bag the packaging, the box, the ribbon, the card, *everything*—if there's a speck of evidence on any of it, I want to know. Starmans, track the box—how it was sent, where it was mailed from, who paid for it. Brooks, Vance, we need DNA on the hair, and we need it yesterday. I don't care who you have to threaten in the lab to get it done, rush it. Locke . . ."

Agent Locke crossed her arms over her chest and gave

Briggs a look. To his credit, he lowered his voice to a more reasonable volume and pitch.

"If this is our UNSUB, it changes everything. We have no evidence that he's ever made contact with a target prior to killing. This may be our chance to get ahead of him."

"We don't even know that this is our UNSUB," Agent Locke pointed out. "It's red hair. For all we know, it could be a prank."

Her gaze drifted over to Lia the second she said the word *prank*. I whipped my head around to look at the Natural liar, too.

Lia tossed her black hair over her shoulder. "This is a little beyond the pale, even for me, Agent Locke."

Locke glanced at me. "Gotten into any arguments lately?" she asked.

I opened my mouth, then glanced at Lia again. *Remind me never to ask you for a favor again.* The venom in her tone when she'd said those words had been palpable.

"Lia." Agent Briggs barely managed to get the word out around his clenched jaw. "Tell me again how you found the present."

Lia's eyes flashed. "I went out to get the mail. There was a package with Cassie's name on it. I opened said package. Inside, there was a box. I decided I wanted to see the look on Cassie's face when *she* opened said box. I brought it into the kitchen. Cassie opened it. The end."

Briggs turned to Locke. "If the DNA comes back as a match for one of our victims, you'll have to completely rework the profile. If it doesn't . . ."

He glanced back at Lia.

"Why does everyone keep looking at me?" she snapped. "I found the package. I didn't send it. If the DNA on the hair doesn't come back as a match, maybe you should think about asking *Cassie* some questions."

"Me?" I asked incredulously.

"You wanted in on this case," Lia retorted. "And now the killer contacts you out of the blue? How lucky for you."

I couldn't tell if Lia believed what she was saying or not. It didn't matter, because Briggs had already turned his diamond-hard gaze on me.

"Cassie didn't do this."

I hadn't even realized that Dean was in the room until he spoke. Clearly, neither had the agents. Briggs actually jumped.

"Cassie's not the type to play games." Dean's voice brooked no doubt. "The entire reason she wanted to work on this case is that she thinks it has something to do with her mother's murder. Why would she risk diverting manpower and resources away from the real investigation when she *knows* the killer is escalating? If this is a prank, it's a prank that's going to get someone killed."

The knot in my chest loosened. I looked at Dean, and suddenly, I could breathe.

"Dean's right." Locke's voice sounded exactly like mine when I was working my way through a puzzle. "If Cassie wanted in on this case, she'd just find a way to keep working it on her own."

I tried very hard not to look conspicuous—because that was *exactly* what I'd been trying to do.

"Cassie, did you or did you not drop this case when I told you to?" Briggs took a step forward, invading my personal space. "Have you done *anything* that might have drawn the killer's attention?"

I shook my head—no to both questions. Briggs's hand fell back to his side. He clenched his jaw again. For the second time, Dean intervened.

"All Cassie did was give a copy of the case file to me."

Every pair of eyes in the room turned to Dean. Normally, he stood and walked like someone who wanted to disappear into the woodwork, but today, his shoulders were back, his jaw set.

"I read the file. I profiled it. And I think Cassie's right." Dean leveled his gaze at Agent Briggs. "These women are stand-ins, and I think there's a very real chance that the person they're standing in for is Cassie's mother."

"You've never even seen the Lorelai Hobbes case file," Briggs shot back. My mother's name hit me like a punch to the stomach.

"I've seen Cassie's mother's picture," Dean argued. "I've

seen the human hair that someone just sent to Cassie as a gift."

Briggs listened to every word Dean had to say, an intense look of concentration on his face. "You're not authorized to work this case," he said finally.

Dean shrugged. "I know."

"You are not *going* to be working this case."

"I know."

"I'm going to pretend that we never had this conversation."

"Liar," Lia coughed.

Briggs was not amused. "You may leave the room, Lia."

Lia clasped her hands together. "Oh, Mother, may I?"

Dean made a choking sound. I wasn't entirely certain, but he might have been swallowing a laugh.

"Now, Lia."

After a long moment and a glare aimed at the room as a whole, Lia twirled on her toes and stalked out of the room. Once he was sure Lia was gone, Agent Briggs turned to Agent Locke. "Do you think this case is related to the Lorelai Hobbes case?"

I didn't flinch when he said my mother's name a second time. I concentrated on the fact that Lia was correct: Briggs had no intention of forgetting what Dean had told him.

I think Cassie's right.

"I don't know that it matters whether the two cases are related or not," Locke answered finally. "Cassie's hair is red.

She's a bit younger than the other victims, but otherwise, she fits the profile of this killer's victims, and more importantly, our UNSUB is escalating. If you assume the last victim's hair was dyed as a message, that means this guy is playing with us. And if he's playing with us, there's a sizable chance that he's *watching* us." Agent Locke rubbed the back of her hand wearily over her brow. "If he's watching us, he could have followed us here, and if he followed us here, he could have seen Cassie."

Briggs's phone rang before he could reply. By the time he hung up, I already knew what the next words out of his mouth were going to be.

"We've got another body."

YOU

You watch the FBI agents scurrying around the crime scene like ants. This particular corpse is not your best work. You killed her last night, and already, her screams have faded from your ears. Her face is still recognizable—more or less.

You used scissors this time instead of your knife.

But that's not the point. Not this time. This time, the point is that the gift you sent sweet little Cassandra Hobbes was the real thing.

The pathetic little slut lying lifeless on the pavement is just a piece of the plan. You abandoned her body at dawn, knowing that it wouldn't be discovered immediately. You'd hoped—prayed, even—that Cassie would be there when the agents got the call.

Did you scream when you opened the box, Cassie? Did you think about me? Am I the thought that keeps you up at night? There's so much you want to ask her.

So much you want to tell her.

The rest of the world will never understand. The FBI will never know the inner workings of your brain.

They'll never know how close you are.

But Cassie—she's going to know everything. The two of you are connected. Cassie is her mother's daughter—and that's as close as you're ever going to get.

wo days later, the hair from the black box came back
as a match for the UNSUB's latest victim.

"I'll accept gifts in lieu of an apology," Lia told
Agent Locke. "Any time now is fine."

Locke didn't reply. The three of us—along with Briggs,
Michael, and Dean—were in Briggs's study. Sloane was
nowhere to be seen.

You sent me a piece of hair. I couldn't keep from talking
to the killer in my head, couldn't keep from thinking about
the present and what it meant that the UNSUB had sent it
to me. *Was she screaming when you cut it off? Did you use
the scissors to cut her afterward? Was it ever even about her?
Or was it about me? About my mother?*

"Am I in danger?" I sounded remarkably calm, like my
question was just a piece of the puzzle and not a matter of
life and death—specifically, mine.

"What do you think?" Locke asked.

Briggs narrowed his eyes, like he couldn't believe she was using this as a teaching opportunity, but I answered the question anyway.

"I think this UNSUB wants to kill me, but I don't think he wants to kill me yet."

"This is insane." Michael had that look on his face—the one that told me he wanted to hit someone. "Cassie, are you even listening to yourself?" He turned to Briggs. "She's in shock."

"*She* is standing right here," I said, but I didn't contradict the rest of Michael's statement. Given his ability to read people, I had to assume that he might be right. Maybe I was in shock. I couldn't deny the fact that my emotions were on lockdown.

I wasn't angry.

I wasn't scared.

I wasn't even thinking about my mother and the fact that this UNSUB might very well have killed her, too.

"You kill women," I said out loud. "Women with red hair. Women who remind you of someone else. And then one day, you see me, and for whatever reason, I'm not like the others. You never needed to talk to them. You never needed them to go to sleep at night thinking about you. But I'm different. You send me a gift—maybe you want to scare me. Maybe you're playing with me or using me to play with the feds.

But the way you wrapped that box, the care you took with my name on the card—there's a part of you that thinks you really *have* given me a gift. You're talking to me. You made me special, and when you kill me, that will have to be special, too." Every single person in the room was staring at me. I turned to Dean. "Am I wrong?"

Dean considered the question. "I've been killing for a long time," he said, slipping into the killer's mind as easily as I had. "And each time, it's a little bit *less* than it was the time before. I don't want to get caught, but I need the danger, the thrill, the challenge." He closed his eyes for a moment, and when he opened them, it was like the two of us were the only two people in the room.

"You're not wrong, Cassie."

"This is sick," Michael said, his voice rising. "There's some psycho out there, fixating on Cassie, and you two are acting like this is some kind of game."

"It *is* a game," Dean said.

I knew Dean wasn't enjoying this, that looking at me through a killer's eyes wasn't something he would have *chosen* to do, but Michael only heard the words. He lunged forward and caught Dean by the front of his shirt.

A second later, Michael had Dean pinned to the wall. "Listen to me, you sick son of a—"

"Michael!" Briggs pulled him off Dean. At the last second, Dean lunged forward and grabbed Michael, reversing their positions and wedging his elbow underneath Michael's throat.

Dean lowered his voice to a whisper. "I never said this was a game to me, Townsend."

It was a game to the UNSUB. I was the prize. And if we weren't careful, Michael and Dean were going to kill each other.

"Enough." Locke put a hand on Dean's shoulder. He stiffened, and for a second, I thought he might hit her.

"Enough," Dean echoed, expelling a breath. He let Michael go and took a step back. Then he just kept walking backward until his back hit the opposite wall. He was a person who didn't lose control, who couldn't afford to, and he'd come close enough with Michael just now that it scared him.

"So what do we do now?" I asked, pulling everyone's attention from Dean and giving him a second to recover.

Briggs jabbed his index finger in my direction. "You're still not working this case. Either of you." He spared a glare for Dean before returning that laser focus to me. "I've assigned a team to watch the house. I'll introduce you all to Agents Starmans, Vance, and Brooks. Until further notice, none of you will be leaving this residence, and Cassie is never alone."

Closing ranks around me wasn't going to bring us any closer to this UNSUB.

"You should take me with you," I told Briggs. "If this guy wants me, we should use that. Set a trap."

"No!" Michael, Dean, and Briggs responded at the exact same time. I turned beseeching eyes to Agent Locke.

She looked like she was on the verge of agreeing with me, but at the last second, she bit her lip and shook her head. "The UNSUB has only made contact once. He'll try again, whether you're here or elsewhere, and at least here, we have the home court advantage."

I'd been taught that there was no such thing as the home court advantage, but my mother's lessons had been geared toward reading people, not playing cat and mouse with killers.

"The UNSUB is breaking pattern." Locke reached out and touched the side of my face softly. "As scary as it is, that's a good thing. We know what he wants, and we can keep him from getting it. The more riled up he gets, the more likely he is to make a mistake."

"I can't just do *nothing*." I locked my eyes onto my mentor's, willing her to understand.

"You can do something," she said finally. "You can make a list. Everyone you've spoken to, everyone you've met, every place you've been, every person who's spent even a second *looking* at you since you got here."

My mind went immediately to the man who'd interrupted my reading that afternoon by the Potomac—without telling me his name. Was that him? Was it nothing?

It was hard not to be paranoid, given what I knew now.

"The UNSUB mailed the package," Lia pointed out, jarring me from my thoughts. "He doesn't have to be local."

Dean jammed his hands into his pockets. "He'd want to see her," he said, his own gaze flicking toward my face, just for a second.

"We weren't able to trace the package," Locke said grimly. "Busy post office, busy day, less than observant mail clerk, and no security cameras. Our UNSUB paid cash, and the return address is obviously faked. This guy is good, and he's playing with us. At this point, I wouldn't rule anything out."

or the next three days, I could barely manage to go to the bathroom without someone else following me in.

And every time I looked out the window, I knew that the FBI was out there, watching and waiting, hoping the killer would try again.

"There are approximately thirty thousand working morticians in the United States."

Sloane—who was the only person in the house I couldn't justify throwing out of my room, since it was her room, too—had pulled Cassie babysitting duty when I'd tried to sneak away for some time alone.

"Morticians?" I repeated. I eyed her suspiciously. "Did someone give you coffee?"

Sloane very pointedly did not answer the coffee question. "I thought you could use a distraction."

I plopped down on my bed. "Don't you have any more cheerful statistics?"

Sloane frowned in contemplation. "Are balloon animals cheerful?"

Oh dear lord.

"Balloonists are more likely than other circus performers to suffer from subconjunctival hemorrhages."

"Sloane, subconjunctival hemorrhages are not cheerful."

She shrugged. "If you had a balloon, I could make you a dachshund."

Another few days of this and I might willingly serve myself up to the UNSUB. Who would have thought my fellow Naturals would take Briggs's decree that I not be left alone so seriously? Dean and Michael could barely stand to be in the same room with each other, but the second I stepped out of my bedroom, one or both of them would be there waiting for me. The only thing that could have made this whole situation more awkward was if Lia hadn't magnanimously decided to stay out of the fray.

"Knock, knock!"

So much for Lia's magnanimousness.

"What do you want?" I asked her, not bothering to sugarcoat my words.

"My, but we're cranky today."

If looks could kill, Lia would have been dead on the floor,

and I would have been on trial for murder.

"I suppose," Lia said, with the air of someone making a most generous concession, "that the argument you had with Dean about his father wasn't entirely your fault, and since this whole hair-in-a-box thing seems to have given him a renewed purpose in life, I'm not morally obligated to make you miserable anymore."

I wasn't sure how to reply to that. "Thank you?"

"I thought you could use a distraction." Lia smiled. "If there's one thing I excel at, it's distractions."

The last time I'd let Lia dictate our plans, I'd ended up kissing Dean *and* Michael in a span of less than twenty-four hours, but after three days of house arrest and way too many statistics about dachshunds, I was desperate.

"What kind of distraction did you have in mind?"

Lia tossed a bag on my bed. I opened it.

"Did you rob a cosmetics store?"

Lia shrugged. "I like makeup—and nothing says distraction like a makeover. Besides . . ." She reached in the bag and pulled out a lipstick. Smiling wickedly, she uncapped it and twisted the bottom. "This is definitely your color."

I eyed the lipstick. The color was dark—halfway between red and brown. Way too sexy for me—and strangely familiar.

"What do you say?" Lia didn't actually wait for an answer. She pushed me into a sitting position on the bed. She leaned into my personal space and tilted my chin back. And then she dragged the lipstick across my lips.

"Kleenex!" Lia barked.

Sloane supplied the Kleenex, a goofy grin on her face.

"Blot," Lia ordered.

I blotted.

"I knew that would be a good color on you," Lia told me, her voice smug and self-satisfied. Without another word, she turned her attention to my eyes. When she was finally finished, I pushed her off me and walked over to the mirror.

"Oh." I couldn't keep the sound from escaping my mouth. My blue eyes looked impossibly big. My lashes had been thoroughly mascara-ed, and the color on my lips was dark against my porcelain skin.

I looked like my mother. My features, the way they came together on my face—everything.

Blue dress. Blood. Lipstick.

A series of images flashed through my mind, and I realized with sudden clarity why the color of this lipstick had seemed so familiar. I turned back to the bed and scavenged through the bag of makeup until I found it. I turned the tube upside down, looking for the color's name.

"*Rose Red*," I read, swallowing after I said the words. I turned to Lia. "Where did you get this?"

"What does it matter?"

My knuckles went white around the tube. "Where did you get this, Lia?"

"Why do you want to know?" she countered, folding her arms over her chest and examining her nails.

"I just do, okay?" I couldn't tell her more than that—and I shouldn't have had to. "Please?"

Lia gathered the makeup off the bed and made her way to the door. She gave me one of those smiles that wasn't a smile. "I bought it, Cassie. With money. As part of our fine system of capitalistic exchange. Happy?"

"The color—" I started to say.

"It's a popular color," Lia cut in. "If you bribe Sloane with some java, she could probably tell you exactly how many millions of tubes of it they sell every year. Seriously, Cassie. Don't ask why. Just say thank you."

"Thanks," I said softly, but I couldn't help feeling that the universe was mocking me, and I couldn't keep from looking down at the tube in my hand and thinking, over and over again, that once upon a time, I'd known someone else who was partial to Rose Red lipstick.

My mother.

YOU

"Hold still."

The girl whimpers, her eyes filling with tears, her hands pulling at the bindings. You backhand her, and she falls to the ground. There's no pleasure to be had in this.

She's not Lorelai.

She's not Cassie.

She's not even a proper imitation. But you had to do something. You had to show the people closing ranks around Cassie what happens when they try to stand between you and what is yours.

"Hold still," you say again.

This time, the girl obeys. You don't kill her. You don't even hurt her.

Not yet.

CHAPTER 30

I woke midmorning to slanting rays of light breaking through my bedroom window. Sloane was nowhere to be seen. After doing a cursory check of the hallway, I slunk into the bathroom and locked the door behind me.

Solitude. For now.

I pulled the shower curtain, stretching it across the length of the tub. With a twist of my wrist, I turned on the spray, as hot as it would go. The sound of water drumming against the porcelain tub was soothing and hypnotic. I sank down to the floor, pulling my knees to my chest.

Six days ago, a serial killer had contacted me, and my only reaction had been to crawl into the UNSUB's head, calm and cool. But last night, wearing the same shade of lipstick as my mother had undone me.

It was a coincidence, I told myself. *A horrible, twisted, untimely coincidence that within days of being contacted by a* killer who might have murdered my mother, Lia had made me up to look just like her.

"It's a popular color. Just say thank you."

Steam built up in the air around me, reminding me that I was wasting hot water, a cardinal sin in a house with five teenagers. I stood and swiped my arm across the mirror, leaving a streak on its steam-covered surface.

I stared at myself, banishing the image of Rose Red on my lips. This was me. I was fine.

Stripping off my pajamas, I stepped into the shower, letting the spray hit me straight in the face. The flashback came suddenly and without warning.

Fluorescent lights flicker overhead. On the ground, my shadow flickers, too.

The door to her dressing room is slightly ajar.

I concentrated on the sound of the water, the feel of it on my skin, pushing back against the memories.

The smell—

Abruptly, I turned off the shower. Wrapping a towel around my torso, I stepped out onto the bath mat, dripping wet. I combed my fingers through my hair and turned to the sink.

That was when I heard the scream.

"Cassie!" It took me a moment to pick out my name, and another after that to recognize that Sloane was the one yelling. Wearing only a towel, I rushed across to our room.

"What? Sloane, what is it?"

She was still clad in her pajamas. White-blond hair stuck to her forehead. "It had my name on it," she said, her voice strained. "It's not stealing if it has my name on it."

"What had your name on it?"

With shaking hands, she held out a padded envelope.

"Who did you *not steal* this from?" I asked.

Sloane looked distinctly guilty. "One of the agents downstairs."

They'd been screening all of our mail, not just mine.

Angling my head so that I could see what was inside the envelope, I realized why Sloane had screamed.

There, inside the envelope, was a small, black box.

Once the box had been removed from the envelope, there was no question that it matched the first one: the ribbon, the bow, the white card with my name written on it in careful, not quite cursive script. The only difference was the size—and the fact that this time, the UNSUB had used Sloane to get to me.

You know the FBI has me under guard. You want me anyway.

"You didn't open the box." Agent Briggs sounded surprised. About ten seconds after I'd realized what was inside the envelope, Agents Starmans and Brooks had burst into the bedroom. They'd called Locke and Briggs. I'd had just enough time to get dressed before the dynamic duo had arrived—with another, older man in tow.

"I didn't want to compromise the physical evidence," I said.

"You did the right thing." The man who'd come with Briggs and Locke spoke for the first time. His voice was gruff, a perfect match for his face, which was weatherworn and suntanned. I put his age at somewhere in the neighborhood of sixty-five. He wasn't tall, but he had a commanding presence, and he looked at me like I was a child.

"Cassie, this is Director Sterling." Locke made the introduction, but the things she didn't say numbered in the dozens.

For instance, she didn't say that this man was their boss.

She didn't say that he was the person who'd signed off on the Naturals program.

She didn't say that he'd been the one to rake Briggs over coals for using Dean on active cases.

She didn't have to.

"I want to be there when you open it." I addressed the words to Agent Locke, but Director Sterling was the one who replied.

"I really don't think that's necessary," he said.

This was a man with children, maybe even grandchildren, even if he was a higher-up at the FBI. I could use that.

"I'm a target," I said, allowing my eyes to go wide. "Keeping this information from me makes me vulnerable. The more I know about this UNSUB, the safer I am."

"We can keep you safe." The director spoke like a man used to having his words taken as law.

"That's what Agent Briggs said four days ago," I said, "and now this guy is coming at me through Sloane."

"Cassie—" Agent Briggs started to talk to me in the same voice the director used—like I was a little kid, like they hadn't brought me here to solve cases in the first place.

"The UNSUB struck again, didn't he?" My question—which was a guess, really—was met with absolute silence.

I was right.

"This UNSUB wants me." I worked my way through the logic. "You tried to keep him away from me. Whatever's in that box, it's a step up from what the UNSUB sent me last time. A warning for you, a present for me. If he thinks you're keeping it from me, things are only going to get worse."

The director nodded to Agent Briggs. "Open the box."

Briggs put on a pair of gloves. He pulled on the edge of the ribbon, and the bow came undone. He set the card to the side and lifted the lid off the box.

White tissue paper.

Carefully, he opened the tissue paper. A ringlet of hair lay in the box. It was blond.

"Open the card," I said, my voice catching in my throat.

Briggs opened the envelope and pulled out a card. Like

the last one, it was white, elegant, but plain. Briggs opened the card, and a photograph fell out.

I caught sight of the girl in the picture before they could obscure it from me. Her wrists were bound behind her body. Her face was swollen, and dried blood had crusted around her scalp. Her eyes were filled with tears and so much fear that I could *hear* her screaming behind the duct-tape gag.

She had dirty blond hair and a baby face.

"She's too young," I said, my stomach twisting. The girl in the picture was fifteen, maybe sixteen—and none of the UNSUB's other victims had been minors.

This girl was younger than me.

"Briggs." Locke picked up the photo and held it out to him. "Look at the newspaper."

I'd been so fixated on the girl's face that I hadn't noticed the newspaper carefully poised against her chest.

"She was alive this time yesterday," Briggs said, and that was when I knew—why this present was different from the last one, why the hair in the box was blond.

"You took her," I said softly, "because they took me."

Locke caught my eye, and I knew she'd heard me. She *agreed* with me. Guilt rose like nausea in the back of my throat. I pushed it down. I could process this later. I could hate the UNSUB—and myself—for the blood and bruises on this girl's face later. But right now, I had to hold it together.

I had to *do* something.

"Who is she?" I asked. If taking this girl was the killer's way of lashing out because the FBI had tried to keep him from me, she wouldn't be just anyone. This girl didn't fit with the victimology of the UNSUB's other victims, but if there was one thing I knew about this killer, it was that he always chose his targets for a reason.

"Ms. Hobbes, I appreciate your personal interest in this case, but that information is above your pay grade."

I gave the director a look. "You don't pay me. And if the killer is watching, and you insist on keeping me locked up out of reach, it's going to get worse."

Why couldn't he see that? Why couldn't Briggs? It was *obvious*. The FBI wanted to keep me out of this, but the killer wanted me in.

"What does the card say?" Locke asked. "The picture is only part of the message."

Briggs looked at me, then at the director. Then he flipped the card around so that we could read it for ourselves.

CASSIE—WON'T IT LOOK BETTER RED?

The implication was clear. This girl was alive. But she wouldn't be for long.

"Who is she?" I asked again.

Briggs kept his mouth clamped shut. He had priorities, and keeping his job was number one.

"Genevieve Ridgerton." Locke answered my question, her voice flat. "Her father is a U.S. senator."

Genevieve. So now the girl the UNSUB had taken because of me, the girl the UNSUB had *hurt* because of me, had a name.

The director took a step toward Locke. "That information is need-to-know, Agent Locke."

She waved off his objection. "Cassie's right. Genevieve was taken as a deliberate strike at us. We put protection on Cassie, we kept her from leaving the house, and this was the direct response. We're no closer to catching this monster than we were four days ago, and he will kill Genevieve unless we give him a reason not to."

He would kill Genevieve because of me.

"What are you suggesting?" The director said those words in a tone brimming with warning, but Locke responded as if the question had been posed in earnest.

"I'm suggesting that we give this killer exactly what he wants. We deal Cassie in. We take her with us and pay another visit to the crime scene."

"You really think she'll find something we missed?"

Locke shot me an apologetic look. "No—but I think that if we take Cassie to the crime scene, the killer might follow."

"We're not training these kids to play bait," Agent Briggs said sharply.

The director turned his attention from Locke to Briggs. "You promised me three cold cases by the end of the year," he said. "So far, your Naturals have delivered one."

I could feel the dynamics in the room shifting. Agent Briggs didn't want to risk something happening to one of his precious Naturals. The director was skeptical that our abilities were worth the cost of this program, and whatever objections he had to bringing a seventeen-year-old to a crime scene must have been outweighed by the fact that this situation could have major political ramifications.

This UNSUB hadn't chosen a senator's daughter by chance.

"Take her with you to the club, Briggs," the director grunted. "If anyone asks, she's a witness." He turned to me. "You don't have to do this if you don't want to, Cassandra."

I knew that. I also knew that I did want to—and not just because Locke might be right about my presence being enough to lure the killer out. I couldn't just sit back and watch this happen.

Behavior. Personality. Environment.

Victimology. MO. Signature.

I was a Natural—and as sick as it was, I had a relationship with this UNSUB. If they brought me to the crime scene, I might see something the others had missed.

"I'll go," I told the director. "But I'm bringing backup of my own."

CHAPTER 31

C lub Muse was an eighteen-and-over establishment. They only served alcohol to patrons wearing twenty-one-plus wristbands. And yet, somehow, Genevieve Ridgerton, who was neither eighteen nor twenty-one, had—according to all witness reports—been more than a little tipsy when she'd disappeared from the Club Muse bathroom three nights earlier.

Director Sterling had reluctantly agreed to allow me to bring two of the others with me to the crime scene, and then he'd put as much distance between us and him as possible. As a result, Briggs and Locke were the ones who escorted me to the club—and they were the ones who'd decided which of my housemates got to tag along.

Sloane was currently walking the inside perimeter of the club, looking for points of entry and doing some sort of calculation involving maximum occupancy, the popularity of the band playing, total amount of alcohol consumed, and the line for the bathroom.

Dean, Locke, and I were tracing Genevieve's last steps.

"Two unisex bathrooms. Dead bolts on each of the doors." Dean's dark eyes scanned the area with almost military precision.

"Genevieve was in line with a friend," Locke told us. "The friend went into Bathroom A, leaving Genevieve next in line. When the friend came out, Genevieve wasn't in line. The friend assumed she was in the second bathroom and went back to the bar. She never saw Genevieve again."

I thought of the Genevieve I'd seen in the UNSUB's picture, the Genevieve with bruises and blood crusted on her scalp. Then I pushed that image out of my head and forced myself to think about the events that had led to her abduction.

"Okay," I said. "So I'm Genevieve. I'm a little drunk, maybe more than a little. I stumble my way through the crowd, wait in line. My friend goes into one of the bathrooms. The next one opens up." I weaved on my feet a bit as I walked through the motions the girl would have taken. "I slip into the bathroom. Maybe I remember to throw the dead bolt. Maybe I don't."

Mulling that over, I scanned the room: a toilet, a sink, a broken mirror. Had the mirror been that way before Genevieve was taken? Or had it gotten broken when she was abducted? I turned three hundred and sixty degrees, taking it all in and trying to ignore just how disgusting the bathrooms at eighteen-and-over clubs really were. The floor was permanently sticky. I didn't even want to look at the toilet, and there was graffiti scrawled across every surface of the bathroom walls.

"If you forgot to bolt the door, I might have followed you in."

It took me a moment to realize that Dean was speaking from the UNSUB's perspective. He took a step toward me, making the small space feel even smaller. I stumbled backward, but there was nowhere to go.

"Sorry," he said, holding his hands up. Channeling Genevieve, I felt my lips curl into a loopy smile. After all, this was a club, and he was kind of cute. . . .

A second later, Dean had his hand over my mouth. "I could have chloroformed you."

I twisted out of his hold, all too aware of how close my body was to his. "You didn't."

"No," he agreed, his eyes on mine. "I didn't."

This time, he wrapped a hand around my waist. I leaned into him.

"Maybe I'm not just a little drunk," I said. "Maybe I'm drunker than I should be."

Dean caught on. "Maybe I slipped a little something extra into your drink."

"It's five feet from the bathroom door to the nearest

emergency exit." Sloane issued that observation from just outside the bathroom door. Clearly, she had better sense than to join the two of us in already cramped—and disgusting—quarters.

That went double for Agent Locke. "We have a witness who can place Genevieve going into this bathroom," she said. "But no one remembers seeing her leave."

Given that Genevieve probably wasn't the only tipsy person in Club Muse that night, I wasn't terribly surprised. It was scary to think how easy it might have been to lead a drugged girl out of the bathroom, down the hallway, and out the door.

"Nine seconds," Sloane said. "Even if you account for a sluggish gait on Genevieve's part, the distance between the bathroom and the closest exit is small enough that someone could have gotten her out of here in nine seconds."

You chose Genevieve. You waited for exactly the right moment. You only needed nine seconds.

This UNSUB was meticulous. A planner.

You do everything for a reason, I thought, *and the reason you took this girl is me.*

"Okay, kiddies, playtime's over." Agent Locke had done an admirable job of fading into the background and letting us work, but clearly, she was on a timetable. "For what it's worth, I reached the same conclusion you did. Two of the previous victims had traces of GHB in their systems. The

UNSUB most likely slipped something into Genevieve's drink and walked her right out the emergency exit with no one the wiser."

Belatedly, I realized that Dean still had his arm wrapped around my waist. A second later, he must have realized the same thing, because he pulled away from me and took a step back.

"Any sign of the UNSUB outside?" he asked.

It was easy to forget that I wasn't actually here as a profiler. I was here as bait, and the FBI was hoping I'd bring the killer straight to them.

"Plainclothes agents are canvassing the streets as we speak," Agent Locke told us, "masquerading as volunteers, handing out flyers, and looking for people who might have information about Genevieve's disappearance."

Dean leaned back against the wall. "But you're really just making a list of the people who approach the agents?"

Locke nodded. "Got it in one. I'm even patching a video feed through to Michael and Lia back at the house so they can analyze anyone who approaches."

Apparently, Locke wasn't above taking advantage of the director's authorization to involve Naturals in this case.

She pushed a strand of stray hair out of her face. "Cassie, we need you to make a few more appearances outside. I'd have you handing out flyers if I thought we could get away with it, but even I'm not willing to push Briggs that far."

I tried to put myself in the UNSUB's shoes. He'd wanted me out of the house; I was out of the house. He'd wanted me involved in this case; now I was standing in the middle of the crime scene.

"Have you seen everything you need to see here?" Agent Locke asked me.

I glanced over at Dean, who was still keeping his distance.

You wanted me involved in this case.

You do everything for a reason.

The reason you took this girl is me.

"No." I didn't explain myself to Agent Locke. I didn't have an explanation. But I knew in my gut that we couldn't leave yet. If this was part of the UNSUB's plan, if the UNSUB had wanted me to come here . . .

"We're missing something."

Something the UNSUB would have expected me to see. Something I was supposed to find, something that was supposed to hold meaning for me.

Slowly, I turned around, taking in the three-sixty view once more. I looked under the sink. I ran my fingers gingerly along the edges of the broken mirror.

Nothing.

Methodically, I raked my eyes over the graffiti on the walls. Initials and hearts, curse words and slurs, doodles, song lyrics . . .

"There." A single line of text caught my eye. At first, I

didn't even read the words. All I saw were the letters: not quite cursive and not quite print, the same hyperstylized handwriting as on the cards that came with each black box.

FOR A GOOD TIME

The sentence cut off there. Frantically, I ran my finger over the wall, sorting through text, looking for that handwriting to pick up again.

CALL 567-3524. GUARANTEED

A phone number. My heart skipped a beat, but I forced myself to keep going: up and down the walls of the bathroom, looking for another line.

Another clue.

I found it near the mirror.

PLUS ONE. KOLA AND THORN.

Kola and Thorn? The more I read, the more the UNSUB's message sounded like gibberish.

"Cassie?" Agent Locke cleared her throat. I ignored her. There had to be more. I started at the top and went through all of the graffiti again. Once I was sure there was nothing else, I walked out of the bathroom to get some air. Locke, Dean, and Sloane had been joined by Agent Briggs.

"We need you to make another appearance outside, Cassie." Agent Briggs clearly considered that an order.

"The UNSUB's not there," I told them.

The FBI thought that by bringing me here, they'd been laying a trap for my killer, but they were wrong. The UNSUB was the one laying a trap for us.

"I need a pen," I said.

After several seconds, Briggs gave me a pen.

"Paper?"

He removed a notebook from his lapel pocket and handed it to me.

"The UNSUB left us a message," I said, but what I really meant was that he'd left *me* a message.

I scrawled the words onto the page, then handed it to Briggs.

"*For a good time, call 567-3524. Guaranteed plus one. Kola and Thorn.*" Briggs lifted his eyes from the page to meet mine. "You're sure this is from the UNSUB?"

"It matches the cards," I told him. The way my name had looked in the killer's script was burned into my mind. "I'm sure."

To them, the cards were evidence. But to me, they were personal. Without even thinking about it, I reached for my cell phone.

"What are you doing?" Dean asked me.

I pressed my lips into a firm line. "Calling the number."

Nobody stopped me.

"I'm sorry, the number you have dialed is not in service. Please try your call again later."

I hung up, looked down at the floor, then shook my head.

"No area code," Sloane said. "Are we thinking DC? Virginia? Maryland? That's eleven possible area codes within a hundred-mile radius."

"Starmans." Agent Briggs was on his cell phone immediately. "I'm going to read you a telephone number. I need you to try it with every area code within a three-hour driving distance of this location."

"Can I see your phone, Cassie?" Sloane's request distracted me from Briggs's conversation. Unsure why she wanted it, I handed her my phone. She stared at it for a minute, her lips moving rapidly, but no sounds coming out. Finally she looked up. "It's not a phone number—or at least, not one you're supposed to call."

I waited for an explanation. She obliged.

"567-3524. On a telephone, five, six, three, two, and four each correspond to three letters on the keypad. Seven is a four-letter number: *P, Q, R,* and *S.* That's two thousand nine hundred and sixteen possible seven-letter combinations for 567-3524."

I wondered how long it would take Sloane to run through the two thousand nine hundred and sixteen possible combinations.

"Lorelai."

"What?" The sound of my mother's name was like a bucket of ice water thrown directly into my face.

"567-3524 is the telephone number that corresponds to the word *Lorelai*. It also spells *lose-lag, lop-flag,* and *Jose-jag,* but the only seven-letter, single-word possibility—"

"Is *Lorelai*." I finished Sloane's sentence and translated the message with that meaning.

For a good time, call Lorelai. Guaranteed plus one. Kola and Thorn.

"Plus one," Dean read over my shoulder. "You think the UNSUB is trying to tell us that we've got another victim on our hands?"

For a good time, call Lorelai.

Now I had ironclad proof that this case had something to do with my mother's. That was why the UNSUB had wanted me to come here. He'd left me this message—complete with a "guaranteed plus one." Someone the UNSUB had already attacked? Someone he was planning on attacking?

I wasn't sure. All I knew was that if I didn't solve this, if *we* didn't solve this, someone else was going to die.

Genevieve Ridgerton. Plus one. How many people are you going to kill because of me? I asked silently.

There was no answer, just the realization that everything was playing out exactly as the UNSUB had intended. Every discovery I'd made had been choreographed. I was playing a part.

Unable to stop myself, I turned my attention to the last line of the message.

Kola and Thorn.

"Symbolism?" Dean asked me, following my thoughts exactly. "Kola. Cola. Drinking. Thorn. Rose. Blood . . ."

"An anagram?" Sloane had that faraway look in her eye, the same one she'd gotten the day I met her, kneeling over a pile of glass. "Ankh onto lard. Hot nodal nark. Land rand hook. Oak land north."

"North Oakland," Dean cut in. "That's in Arlington."

For a good time, call Lorelai. Guaranteed plus one. North Oakland.

"We need a list of every building on North Oakland," I said, my body buzzing with a sudden rush of adrenaline.

"What are we looking for?" Briggs asked me.

I didn't have an answer—a warehouse, maybe, or an abandoned apartment. I tried to focus, but I couldn't quite rid my brain of the sound of my mother's name, and I realized suddenly that if this killer knew me half as well as he thought he did, there was another possibility.

For a good time, call Lorelai.

The dressing room. The blood. I swallowed. "I'm not sure," I said. "But I think you might be looking for a theater."

CHAPTER 32

"We've got a body at a small, independent theater in Arlington." Agent Briggs's fingers curled into his palms as he delivered the news, but he fought the urge to clench his fists. "It's not Genevieve Ridgerton."

I didn't know whether to be relieved or upset. Somewhere, fifteen-year-old Genevieve might still be alive. But now we were dealing with body number eight.

Our UNSUB's "plus one."

"Starmans, Vance, Brooks: I want the three of you to take the kids back to the house. I want one of you posted at the front door, one at the back door, and one with Cassie at all times." Agent Briggs turned and started walking out of the club, a signal to the rest of us that he was so confident that we would follow his orders that he didn't even need to stay here to see them through.

I didn't need Lia or Michael here to tell me that his confidence was a lie.

"I'm going with you," I said, following him outside. "The exact same logic that let you bring me here applies in Arlington. The UNSUB turned this into a little treasure hunt. He wants to see me follow it to the end."

"I don't care what he wants," Briggs cut in. "I want to keep you safe."

His tone was uncompromising and full of warning, but I couldn't stop myself from asking, "Why? Because I'm *valuable*? Because Naturals work so well as a team, and you'd hate to throw that off?"

Agent Briggs closed the space between us and brought his face down level with mine. "Do you really think that little of me?" he asked quietly. "I'm ambitious. I'm driven. I'm single-minded, but do you really think that I would knowingly put any of you in danger?"

I thought of the moment we'd met. The pen without the cap. His preference for basketball over golf.

"No," I said. "But we both know that this case is killing you. It's killing Locke, and now there's a senator's daughter involved. If it weren't for me, you wouldn't have sent someone to check out that theater. We wouldn't have discovered the body for hours, maybe days—and who knows what our UNSUB would have done to Genevieve in the meantime?

If you don't want to use me as bait anymore, fine. But you need to take me with you. You need to take all three of us with you, because we might see something that you can't."

That was the whole reason Briggs had started the Naturals program. The whole reason that he'd come to twelve-year-old Dean. No matter how long they did this job, or how much training they had, these agents would never have instincts as finely honed as ours.

"Let her come." Locke placed a hand on Briggs's arm, and for the first time, I wondered if there was anything between the two of them other than work. "If Cassie's old enough to play bait, she's old enough to learn from the experience." Locke glanced at me—at Sloane and Dean. "They all are."

Forty-five minutes later, we pulled up to 4587 North Oakland Street. The local police were already there, but at the FBI's insistence, they hadn't touched a thing. Dean, Sloane, and I waited in the car with Agents Starmans and Vance until the local PD had been cleared off the scene, and then they brought us up to the third floor.

To this tiny theater's only dressing room. I made it halfway down the hall before Agent Briggs stepped out of the room, blocking the entrance.

"You don't need to see this, Cassie," he said.

I could smell it—not rotten, not yet, but coppery: rust with just a hint of decay. I pushed past Briggs. He let me.

The room was rectangular. There was blood smeared across the light switch, blood pooled near the door. The entire left-hand side of the room was lined with mirrors, like a dance studio.

Like my mother's dressing room.

My limbs felt heavy all of a sudden. My lips were numb. I couldn't breathe, and just like that, I was right back—

The door is slightly ajar. I push it open. There's something wet and squishy beneath my feet, and the smell—

I grope for the light switch. My fingers touch something warm and sticky on the wall. Frantically, I search for the light switch—

Don't turn it on. Don't turn it on. Don't turn it on.

I turn it on.

I'm standing in blood. There's blood on the walls, blood on my hands. A lamp lies shattered on the wood floor. A desk is upturned, and there's a jagged line in the floorboards.

From the knife.

Pressure on my shoulders forced me to stop reliving the memory. Hands. Dean's hands, I realized. He brought his face very close to mine.

"Stay in control," he said, his voice steady and warm. "Every time you go back there, every time you see it—it's just blood, just a crime scene, just a body." He dropped his hands to his sides. "That's all it is, Cassie. That's all you can let it be."

I wondered which memories he relived over and over—wondered about the bodies and the blood. But right now, in this moment, I was just glad that he was here, that I wasn't alone.

I took his advice. I forced myself to look at the mirror, smeared with blood. I could make out handprints, finger tracks, like the victim had used the mirror to pull herself along the ground after she was too weak to walk.

"Time of death was late last night," Briggs said. "We'll have Forensics in here to see if they can lift any fingerprints besides the victim's off the mirror."

"That's not her blood."

I glanced over at Sloane and realized that she was kneeling next to the body. For the first time, I looked at the victim. Her hair was red. She'd obviously been stabbed repeatedly.

"The medical examiner will tell you the same thing," Sloane continued. "This woman is five feet tall, approximately a hundred and ten pounds. Given her size, we're looking at death from exsanguination with the loss of three quarts of blood, maybe less. She's wearing jeans and a cashmere top. Cashmere—and other forms of wool—can absorb up to thirty percent of its weight in moisture without even appearing damp. Since the deepest wounds are concentrated over her stomach and chest areas, and her top and jeans were both tight, she'd have had to bleed *through* the fabric before dripping all over the floor."

I looked at the woman's clothes. Sure enough, they were soaked with blood.

"By the time her clothes were saturated enough to leave a puddle of that size on the floor over there"—Sloane gestured toward the door—"our victim wouldn't have been conscious to fight off her attacker, let alone lead him on a merry chase through the room. She's too small, she doesn't have enough blood, the fabrics she's wearing don't expel liquid quickly enough—the numbers don't add up."

"She's right." Agent Briggs stood up from examining the floor. "There's a knife mark on the floor over here. If it was made with a bloody knife, there would be blood embedded in the scratch, but there's not, meaning that either the UNSUB missed at his first attempt at stabbing the woman—which certainly doesn't seem likely, given her size and the fact that he would have had the element of surprise—or the UNSUB deliberately made these marks with a clean knife."

I put myself in the victim's shoes. She was eight or nine inches shorter than my mother's five-nine, but that didn't mean she couldn't have fought. But even if the UNSUB had come after her in the exact same way, what were the chances that the scene would have looked this much like my mother's dressing room? The mirrors on the wall, the blood smeared on the light switch, the dark liquid pooled by the door.

Something about this didn't feel right.

"She's left-handed."

I turned to look at Dean, and he continued, "Victim's wearing her watch on her right hand, and her manicure is more chipped on her left hand than her right," he said. "Was your mother left-handed, Cassie?"

I shook my head and realized where he was going with this. "They wouldn't have fought off an attacker in the same way," I said.

Dean gave a brief nod of agreement. "If anything, we'd expect spatter on this wall." He gestured to the plain wall opposite the mirrors. It was clean.

"The UNSUB didn't kill her here." Locke was the first one who said it out loud. "There's virtually no blood pooled around the body. She was killed somewhere else."

You killed her. You brought her here. You painted the room in blood.

"For a good time, call Lorelai," I murmured.

"Cassie?" Agent Locke raised an eyebrow at me. I answered the question that went along with the eyebrow raise.

"She's just a prop," I said, looking at the woman, wishing I knew her name, wishing that I could still make out the features of her face. "This is a set. This entire thing was staged to look like my mother's death. Exactly like it." My stomach twisted sharply.

"Okay," Agent Locke said. "So I'm the killer. I'm fixated on you, and I'm fixated on your mother. Maybe she was my first kill, but this time, it isn't about your mother."

"It's about you." Dean picked up where Agent Locke had left off. "I'm not trying to relive her death. I'm trying to force you to relive discovering her."

The UNSUB had wanted me here. The presents, the coded message, and now this—a corpse dumped in a crime scene strikingly like my mother's.

"Briggs." One of Briggs's agents—Starmans—stuck his head into the room. "Medical examiner and the forensics team are here. Do you want me to hold them off?"

Briggs looked at Dean, at me, and then at Sloane, still kneeling next to the body. We'd been careful not to touch anything or disturb the crime scene, but plopping three teenagers down in the middle of a murder investigation wasn't exactly covert. Briggs, Locke, and their team obviously knew about us, but I wasn't convinced that the rest of the FBI did, and Briggs confirmed that when he glanced from Starmans to Locke.

"Get them out of here, Starmans," Briggs said. "I want you, Brooks, and Vance rotating through on Cassie's protection detail. Director Sterling has offered some of his best men for surveillance. They'll keep an eye on the house from the outside, but I want one of you with Cassie at all times, and tell Judd that the house arrest is still in effect. No one leaves that house until this killer is caught."

I didn't fight the orders.

I didn't fight to stay there in the room, looking for clues.

There weren't any. This was never about me figuring out who this killer was. This was always, always about the UNSUB playing with me, forcing me to relive the worst day of my life.

Sloane slipped an arm around my waist. "There are fourteen varieties of hugs," she said. "This is one of them."

Locke put a hand on my shoulder and steered the two of us out of the room, Dean on our heels.

This is a game. I heard Dean's voice echoing through my memory. *It's always a game.* That was what he'd told Michael, and at the time, I'd agreed. To the killer, this was a game— and suddenly, I couldn't help thinking that the good guys might not win this one.

We might lose.

I might lose.

CHAPTER 33

I wasn't allowed to go into the house until Judd and the agents on my protection detail had swept it, and even then, Agent Starmans accompanied me to my bedroom.

"You okay?" he asked, giving me a sidelong glance.

"Fine," I replied. It was a stock answer, perfected around the Sunday night dinner table. I was a survivor. Whatever life threw at me, I came out okay, and the rest of the world thought I was great. I'd been faking things for so long that, until the past few weeks with Michael, Dean, Lia, and Sloane, I'd forgotten what it was like to be real.

"You're a tough kid," Agent Starmans told me.

I wasn't in the mood to talk, and I especially wasn't in the mood to be patted metaphorically on the head. All I wanted was to be left alone and given a chance to process, to recover.

"You're divorced," I replied. "Sometime within the past four years, maybe five. Long enough ago that you should have moved on."

I normally made it a rule not to take the things I deduced about people and turn them into weapons, but I needed space. I needed to *breathe*. I stood and walked over to the window. Agent Starmans cleared his throat.

"What do you think the UNSUB is going to do?" I asked wearily. "Take me out with a sniper rifle?"

Not this killer. He'd want up close and personal. You didn't have to be a Natural profiler to see that.

"Why don't you cut the poor agent some slack, Colorado? I'm fairly certain making grown men cry is Lia's specialty, not yours." Michael didn't bother knocking before entering the room and giving Agent Starmans his most charming smile.

"I'm not making anyone cry," I said mutinously.

Michael turned his gaze on me. "Underneath your ticked-off-that-they-won't-leave-me-alone-and-even-more-ticked-off-that-I'm-scared-to-actually-be-alone exterior, I detect a slight trace of guilt, which suggests that you *did* say something below the belt, and you're feeling the tiniest bit bad for using your powers for evil, and *he*"—Michael jerked his head toward Agent Starmans—"is fighting down-turned lips and furrowed eyebrows. I don't need to tell you what that means, do I?"

"Please don't," Agent Starmans muttered.

"Of course, there's also his posture, which suggests some level of sexual frustration—"

Agent Starmans took a step forward. He towered over Michael, but Michael just kept smiling, undeterred.

"No offense."

"I'll be out in the hall," Agent Starmans said. "Keep the door open."

It took me a moment after the agent retreated to realize that Michael had put him on the spot on purpose.

"Were you really reading his posture?" I whispered.

Michael ducked his head next to mine, a delightfully wicked smile on his face. "Unlike you, I have no problems using my ability for nefarious purposes." He reached up and ran his thumb over the edge of my lip and onto my cheek. "You have something on your face."

"Liar."

He brushed his thumb over my other cheek. "I never lie about a pretty girl's face. You're carrying so much tension in yours that I have to ask: should I be worried about you?"

"I'm fine," I said.

"Liar," Michael whispered back.

For a second, I could almost forget everything that had happened today: Genevieve Ridgerton; the coded message on the bathroom wall; the UNSUB butchering a woman and using her body as a prop to recreate my mother's death; the fact that all of this killer's actions were designed to manipulate me.

"You're doing it again," Michael said, and this time, he ran the middle and index fingers of each hand along the lines of my jaw.

In the hallway, Agent Starmans took a step back. And then another, until he was almost out of sight.

"Are you touching me just to make him uncomfortable?" I asked Michael, keeping my voice low enough that the agent wouldn't overhear.

"Not *just* to make him uncomfortable."

My lips twitched. Even the possibility of a smile felt foreign on my face.

"Now," Michael said, "are you going to tell me what happened today, or do I have to drag it out of Dean?"

I gave him a skeptical look. Michael amended his previous statement. "Are you going to tell me what happened today, or am I going to have to have Lia drag it out of Dean?"

Knowing Lia, she'd probably managed to pry at least half of the story out of Dean already—and with my luck, she would pass it on to Michael with embellishments. It was better that he heard it from me—so I started at the beginning with Club Muse and the message on the bathroom wall and didn't stop until I'd told him about the crime scene in Arlington and its resemblance to my mother's.

"You think the similarity was intentional," Michael said.

I nodded. Michael didn't ask me to elaborate, and I realized how much of our conversation happened in silence, with him reading my face and me knowing exactly how he'd respond.

"The theory is that the UNSUB staged all of this for me," I said finally. "It wasn't about the UNSUB reliving the kill. It was about making *me* relive it."

Michael stared at me. "Say the second sentence again."

"It wasn't about the UNSUB reliving the kill," I repeated.

"There," Michael said. "Every time you say the words *reliving the kill*, you duck your head slightly to the right. It's like you're shaking your head or being bashful or . . . *something*."

I opened my mouth to tell him that he was wrong, that he was reading too much into that single sentence, but I couldn't form the words, because he was right. I didn't know why I felt like I was missing something, but I did. If Michael had seen some hint of that in my facial expression . . .

Maybe my body knew something that I didn't.

"It wasn't about the UNSUB reliving the kill," I said again. That was true. I knew it was true. But now that Michael had pointed it out, I could feel my gut telling me, loud and clear, that it wasn't the whole truth.

"I'm missing something." The horror at the crime scene

had been familiar. Almost too familiar. What kind of killer remembered the details of a crime scene so exactly? The splatter, the blood on the mirrors and the light switch, the knife marks on the floor . . .

"Tell me what you're thinking." Michael's words penetrated my thoughts. I focused on his hazel eyes. Out of the corner of my eye, I saw a shadow in the doorway. Agent Starmans. Had he overheard us? Was he *trying* to overhear us?

Michael grabbed my neck. He pulled me toward him. When Agent Starmans glanced in the room, all he saw was Michael and me.

Kissing.

The kiss in the pool was nothing compared to this. Then, our lips had barely brushed. Now, my lips were opening. Our mouths were crushed together. His hand traveled from my neck down to my lower back. My lips tingled, and I leaned into the kiss, shifting my body until I could feel the heat from his in my arms, my chest, my stomach.

On some level, I was aware of the fact that Agent Starmans had hightailed it back down the hall, leaving me alone with Michael. On some level, I was aware of the fact that now was not a time for kissing, of the vortex of emotion I felt when I looked at Michael, of the sound of someone else coming down the hallway.

My fingers curled into claws. I dug them into his T-shirt, his hair. And then finally—finally—I realized what I was doing. What we were doing.

I pulled back, then hesitated. Michael dropped his hands from my back. There was a soft smile on his face, a look of wonderment in his eyes. This was Michael without layers. This was Michael and me—and Dean was standing in the doorway.

"Dean." I forced myself not to scramble backward, not to lean away from Michael in any way. I wouldn't do that to him. The kiss might have started as a distraction, he might have taken advantage of the moment, but I'd kissed him back, and I wasn't going to turn around and make him feel like nothing just because Dean was standing in the doorway and there was something there between him and me, too.

Michael had never made any secret of the fact that he was pursuing me. Dean had fought any attraction he felt for me every step of the way.

"We need to talk," Dean said.

"Whatever you have to say," Michael drawled, "you can say in front of me."

I gave Michael a look.

"Whatever you have to say, you can say in front of me, unless Cassie wishes to speak to you privately, in which case

I completely respect her right to do so," Michael corrected himself.

"No," Dean said. "Stay. It's fine."

He didn't sound fine—and if I was picking up on that, I didn't want to know how easy it was for Michael to see what Dean was feeling.

"I brought you this," Dean said, holding out a file. At first, I thought it was the case file for our UNSUB, but then I saw the label on the file. LORELAI HOBBES.

"My mother's file?"

"Locke snuck me a copy," Dean said. "She thought there might be something here, and she was right. The attack on your mother was poorly planned. It was emotional. It was messy. And what we saw today—"

"Wasn't any of those things," I finished. Dean had just put into words the feeling I'd been on the verge of explaining to Michael. A killer could grow and change, their MO could develop, but the emotions, the rage, the titillation— that didn't just go away. Whoever had attacked my mom would have been too overwhelmed by adrenaline to commit the minutiae of the scene to memory.

The person responsible for the blood in my mother's dressing room five years ago wouldn't have been able to reenact her murder so coldly today.

This wasn't about reliving a kill.

"Even if I'm evolving," Dean said, "even if I've gotten good at what I do—seeing you, Cassie, seeing your mother *in* you, I'd be frenzied." Dean slipped a picture of my mother's crime scene out of the folder. Then he laid a second picture down next to it, of the scene today. Looking at the two photos side by side, I accepted what my gut was telling me, what Dean was telling me.

If you were the one who killed my mother, I told the UNSUB, *if every woman you've killed since is a way to relive that moment, wouldn't her death mean something to you? How could you possibly stage a scene like that and not lose control?*

The UNSUB responsible for the corpse I'd seen today was meticulous. Methodical. The type who needed to be in control and always had a plan.

The person who'd killed my mother was none of those things.

How is that even possible? I wondered.

"Look at the light switches."

I turned around. Sloane was directly behind me, staring at the pictures. Lia entered the room a moment later.

"I took care of Agent Starmans," she said. "He has somehow developed the impression that he is urgently needed in the kitchen." Dean gave her an exasperated look. "What?" she said. "I thought Cassie might want some privacy."

I didn't really think five people counted as "privacy," but I was too stuck on Sloane's words to nitpick Lia's. "Why am I looking at the light switches?"

"There's a single smear of blood on the light switch and plate in both photos," Sloane said. "But in this one"—she gestured to the photo of the scene today—"the blood is on the top of the switch. And in this one, it's on the bottom."

"And the translation, for those of us who don't spend hours working on physical simulations in the basement?" Lia asked.

"In one of the photos, the light switch got smeared with blood when someone with bloody hands turned it off," Sloane said. "But in the other one, it happened when the light was turned on."

My fingers touch something warm and sticky on the wall. Frantically, I search for the light switch. My fingers find it. I don't care that they're covered in warm, wet liquid.

I. Need. It. On.

"I turned the light on," I said. "When I came back to my mother's dressing room—there was blood on my hands when I turned the light on."

But if there had only been one smear of blood on the switch, and that smear of blood was from *my* hand . . .

My mother's killer wouldn't have known it was there. The only people who would have known about the blood on the light switch were the people who'd seen the crime scene *after* I'd returned to the dressing room. After I'd turned the light on. After I'd accidentally coated the switch in blood.

And yet, our UNSUB, who had meticulously recreated my mother's murder scene, had included that detail.

You weren't reliving the kill, I thought, allowing myself to finally give life to the words, *because you weren't the one who killed my mother.*

But who else could this UNSUB—who was unquestionably fixated on my mom, on me—possibly be? My mind raced through the day's events.

The gift, sent to me, but addressed to Sloane.

Genevieve Ridgerton.

The message on the bathroom wall.

The theater in Arlington.

Every detail had been planned. This killer had known exactly what I would do at every step along the way—but not just me. He'd known what *all* of us would do. He'd known that sending a package to Sloane was his best chance of getting it to me. He'd known that Briggs and Locke would cave and bring me to the crime scene. He'd known that I'd find the message, and that someone else would decode it. He'd known that we would find the theater in Arlington, that the agents would let me see it.

"The code," I said, backtracking out loud. The others looked at me. "The UNSUB left a message for me, but I couldn't have decoded it. Not alone." If the UNSUB was so set on forcing me to relive my mother's murder, why leave a message I might not be able to understand?

Had the UNSUB known Sloane would be there? Did he expect her to decode it? Did he know what she could do? And if he did . . .

You know about my mother's case. What if you know about the program, too?

"Lia, the lipstick." I tried to keep my voice steady, tried not to let the panic in my chest worm its way to the surface. "The Rose Red lipstick—where did you get it?"

A few days ago, it had seemed benign: a cruel irony, but nothing more. Now—

"Lia?"

"I told you," Lia said, "I bought it."

I hadn't recognized the lie the first time around.

"Where did you get it, Lia?"

Lia opened her mouth to dish out a retort, then closed it again. Her eyes studied mine. "It was a gift," she said quietly. "I don't know from who. Someone left a bag of makeup on my bed last week. I just assumed I had a makeup fairy." She paused. "Honestly, I thought it might be from Sloane."

"I haven't stolen makeup in months." Sloane's eyes were wide. My stomach lurched.

There was a chance that the UNSUB knew about the program.

The only people who would have been able to reconstruct my mother's crime scene so exactly, the only people who would have known about the blood on the light switch, were people who had access to the crime-scene photos.

And someone had left a tube of my mother's favorite lipstick on Lia's bed.

Inside our house.

CHAPTER 34

"Cassie?" Lia was the first one to break the silence. "Are you okay? You look . . . not good."

I was going to go out on a limb and guess that was about as diplomatic as Lia got.

"I need to call Agent Briggs," I said, and then I paused. "I don't have his number."

Dean fished his phone out of his pocket. "There are only four numbers in my contacts," he said. "Briggs is one of them."

The other three were Locke, Lia, and Judd. My hands shaking, I dialed Agent Briggs.

No answer.

I called Locke.

Please answer. Please answer. Please, please answer.

"Dean?"

Like Agent Briggs, Locke didn't bother with hello.

"No," I said. "It's me."

"Cassie? Is everything okay?"

"No," I said. "It isn't."

"Are you alone?"

"No."

Locke must have heard something in my voice, because she flipped into agent mode in a heartbeat. "Can you talk openly?"

I heard steps in the hallway. Agent Starmans opened the door without knocking, glared pointedly at Lia, then resumed standing guard, right outside the door.

"Cassie," Locke said sharply. "Can you talk?"

"I don't know."

I didn't know anything except for the fact that there was a very real possibility that the killer had been inside our house—for all I knew, the killer could be inside the house now. If the UNSUB had access to FBI files, if he had access to *us* . . .

"Cassie, I need you to listen to me. Hang up the phone. Tell whoever's around you that I'm in the middle of something and I'll stop by the house as soon as I'm done. Then take the phone, go to the bathroom, and call me back."

I did what she told me to do. I hung up the phone. I repeated her words to the rest of the room—and to Agent Starmans, who was standing right outside.

"What did she say?" Lia asked, her eyes locked on to my

face, ready to call me out the second a lie passed my lips.

"She said, 'I'm in the middle of something, and I'll stop by the house as soon as I'm done.'"

Technically, Agent Locke *had* said those exact words. I wasn't lying—and I'd just have to take the chance that Lia wouldn't pick up any cues that I was withholding a chunk of the truth.

"Are you okay?" Dean asked.

"I'm going to the bathroom," I said, hoping they'd read that as me not wanting to admit that I wasn't okay. I walked out of the room without ever looking Michael in the eye.

The second I closed the bathroom door behind me, I locked it. I turned on the sink faucet, and then I called Agent Locke back.

"I'm alone," I said softly, letting the sound of running water mask my words for everyone but her.

"Okay," Locke said. "Now, take a deep breath. Stay calm. And tell me what's wrong."

I told her. She cursed softly under her breath.

"Did you call Briggs?" she asked.

"I tried," I said. "He's not picking up his phone."

"Cassie, I need to tell you something, and I want you to promise me that you're going to keep it together. Briggs is in a meeting with Director Sterling. We have reason to believe that there might be a leak in our unit. Until we get firm evidence to the contrary, we have to assume that your protection detail has been compromised. I need you to get out: quietly, quickly, and without drawing anyone's attention."

I thought about Agent Starmans, out in the hallway, and about the other agents downstairs. I'd been so caught up in the case I hadn't paid attention to them.

To any of them.

"I'll call Starmans and the others," Locke said. "I should be able to buy you a few minutes unguarded."

"I have to get out of here," I said. The idea that the UNSUB might be one of the people who was supposed to protect me—

"You have to calm down," Locke said, her voice firm. "You live in a house full of very perceptive people. If you panic, they'll know it."

Michael. She was talking about Michael.

"He doesn't have anything to do with this," I said.

"I never said he did," Locke replied, "but I've known Michael for longer than you have, Cassie, and he's got a history of doing stupid things for girls. The last thing we need right now is someone playing hero."

I thought of the way that Michael had slammed Dean into the wall when Dean had called the killer's obsession with me a game. I thought of Michael in the pool, telling me about a time when he'd lost it.

"I have to go," I said. The farther away I was from Michael, the safer he'd be. If I left, the UNSUB would follow. We could flush this psychopath out. "I'll call you once I'm clear."

"Cassie, if you hang up this phone and do something stupid," Locke said, channeling Nonna and my mother and Agent Briggs all at once, "I will spend the next five years of your life making sure you deeply, *deeply* regret it. I want you to find Dean. If anyone in that house knows how to spot a killer, it's him, and I trust him to keep you safe. He knows the combination to the safe in Briggs's study. Tell him I said to use it."

It took me a moment to realize that the safe in question must be a gun safe.

"Get to Dean and get out of the house, Cassie. Don't let anyone else see you leave. I'll send the coordinates of our DC safe house. Briggs and I will meet you there."

I nodded, knowing that she couldn't see me, but unable to form intelligible words.

"Stay. Calm."

I nodded again and finally managed to say, "Okay."

"You can do this," Agent Locke said. "You and Dean are an incredible team, and I'm not going to let anything happen to either of you."

Three sharp raps on the bathroom door made me jump, but I forced myself to follow Locke's primary directive and stay calm. I could do this. I had to do this. Hanging up the phone, I stuffed it into my back pocket, turned the faucet off, and glanced at the door.

"Who is it?"

"It's me."

Michael. I cursed inside, because there was calm and there was *calm*, and with Michael's knack for emotions, he'd know in a heartbeat if I was faking.

Calm. Calm. Calm.

I couldn't be angry. I couldn't be scared. I couldn't be panicked or guilty or show any signs that I'd just talked to Agent Locke—not if I wanted to keep Michael out of this. At the last second, as I opened the door, I realized that I wasn't going to be able to do it.

He was going to realize that something was wrong—so I did the only thing I could think of to do. I opened the door, and I lied.

"Look," I said, allowing the bevy of emotions I'd been holding back to show on my face, allowing him to see how tired I was, how overwhelmed, how upset. "If this is about the kiss, I really just cannot deal with this right now." I paused and let those words sink in. "I can't deal with you."

I saw it the second the words hit their mark, because Michael's facial expression utterly changed. He didn't look angry or sad—he looked like he couldn't have cared less. He looked like the boy I'd met in the diner: layers upon layers, mask upon mask.

I brushed past him before he could see that it hurt me to hurt him. Hitting the final nail in the coffin, I stalked down the hallway, knowing he was watching me, and I walked right up to Dean.

"I need your help," I said, my voice low.

Dean glanced over my shoulder. I knew he was looking at Michael. I knew Michael was glaring at him, but I didn't turn around.

I couldn't let myself turn around.

Dean nodded, and a second later, I followed him up to the third floor, to his room. True to Agent Locke's words, Agent Starmans received a phone call that kept him from following.

"Sorry—" I started to say, but Dean cut me off.

"Don't apologize," he said. "Just tell me what you need."

I thought of the way he'd looked, walking in on Michael and me. "Locke wants me out of the house," I said. "Either there's a leak in the FBI and the UNSUB has a way in, or the UNSUB is already here and we just don't know it. Locke said to tell you to use the combination to the safe in the study."

Dean's phone buzzed. A new text.

"That will be the location to the safe house," I said. "I don't know how we're supposed to get down to the study and out of the house without anyone seeing us, but—"

"I do." Dean kept things simple: no more words than absolutely necessary. "There's a back staircase. They blocked it off years ago: too unsteady. Nobody but Judd even knows it's there. If we can get down to the basement, I know a way out. Here." He threw me a sweatshirt off his bed. "Put this on. You're freezing."

It was the middle of summer. In Virginia. I shouldn't have been freezing, but my body was doing its best to go into shock. I slipped the sweatshirt on as Dean ushered me down the back staircase and into the study. I kept watch at the door as he knelt next to the safe.

"Do you know how to shoot?" he asked me.

I shook my head. That particular skill hadn't been part of my mother's training. Maybe if it had been, she'd have still been alive.

Dean loaded one of the guns and tucked it into the waistband of his jeans. He left the other one where it was and shut the safe. Two minutes later, we'd made it to the basement, and a minute after that, we were on our way to the safe house.

YOU

You weren't supposed to make mistakes. The plan was supposed to be perfect. And for a few hours, it was.

But you messed it up. You always mess everything up—and there His voice is again in your head, and you're thirteen years old and cowering in the corner, wondering if it will be fists or his belt or a poker from the fire.

And the worst thing is, you're alone. Surrounded by people or throwing your hands up to protect your face, it doesn't matter. You're always alone.

That's why you can't mess this up. That's why it has to be perfect from here on out. That's why you have to be perfect.

You can't lose Cassie. You won't.

You'll love her, or you'll kill her, but either way, she's going to be yours.

CHAPTER 35

The safe house looked like any other house. Dean went in first. He pulled his gun and held it expertly in front of his body as he cleared the foyer, the living room, the kitchen. I stayed close behind him. We'd made our way back to the foyer when the knob on the front door began to turn.

Dean stepped forward, pushing me further back. He held the gun out steadily. I waited, praying that it was Briggs and Locke on the other side of the door. The hinges creaked. The door slowly opened.

"Michael?"

Dean lowered his weapon. For a split second, I felt a burst of relief, warm and sure, radiating out from the center of my body. I expelled the breath caught in my throat. My heart started to beat again.

And then I saw the gun in Michael's hand.

"What are you doing here?" I asked. Looking at him, at

the gun, I felt like the stupid girl in the horror movie, the one who couldn't see what was right in front of her face. The one who went to check on the radiator in the basement when there was a masked murderer on the loose.

Michael was here.

Michael had a gun.

The UNSUB had a source on the inside.

No.

"Why do you have a gun?" I asked dumbly. I couldn't keep from taking a step toward Michael, even though I couldn't quite read the look on his face.

In front of me, Dean raised his right arm, gun in hand. "Put it down, Townsend."

Michael was going to put down the gun. That was what I told myself. He was going to put down the gun, and this was all going to be some kind of mistake. I'd seen Michael on the verge of violence. He'd told me himself that the potential for losing it was in him, but I *knew* Michael. He wasn't dangerous. He wasn't a killer. The boy I knew wasn't just a mask worn by someone who knew how to manipulate emotions as well as he could read them.

This was Michael. He called me Colorado, and he read Jane Austen, and I could still feel his lips on mine. He was going to put down the gun.

But he didn't. Instead, he lifted it up, training the weapon on Dean.

The two of them stared at each other. Sweat trickled down the back of my neck. I took a step forward, then another one. I couldn't stay in the background.

Michael had a gun trained on Dean.

Dean had a gun trained on Michael.

"I'm warning you, Michael. Put it down." Dean sounded calm. Absolutely, utterly calm in a way that made my stomach churn, because I knew suddenly that he *could* pull the trigger. He wouldn't second-guess himself. He wouldn't hesitate.

If he thought I was in danger, he would put a bullet in Michael's head.

"You put it down," Michael replied. "Cassie—"

I cut Michael off. I couldn't listen to a word either of them had to say, not when we were a hair's breadth away from disaster. "Put it down, Michael," I said. "Please."

Michael's gaze wavered. For the first time, he looked from Dean to me, and I saw it the moment he realized that I wasn't afraid of Dean. That I was afraid of *him*.

"You were gone. Dean was gone. One of Briggs's guns was gone." Michael took a ragged breath. The guarded expression fell from his face, bit by bit, until I was looking at the boy I'd kissed: confused and hurting, longing for me, terrified for me, breakable. "I would never hurt you, Cassie."

Something came undone inside of me. This was Michael—the same Michael he'd always been.

Beside me, Dean repeated his command for Michael to lower the gun. Michael closed his eyes. He lowered his weapon, and the second he did, the sound of gunfire tore through the air.

One shot. Two shots.

My ears ringing, my gut twisting, bile rising in my throat, I tried to figure out which gun had gone off. Michael's hand was by his side. His mouth opened in a tiny O, and I watched with horror as red blossomed across his pale blue shirt. He'd been hit. Twice. Once in the shoulder. Once in the leg. His eyes rolled back in his head. The gun dropped from his fingertips.

He fell.

I turned to see Dean with the gun still in his hand. He was aiming at me.

No. No no no no no no no.

And that was when I heard a voice behind me and realized that Dean wasn't the one holding the gun that had gone off. He wasn't aiming at me. He was aiming at the person standing *behind* me. The one who'd shot Michael.

He was aiming at Special Agent Lacey Locke.

PART FOUR: SEEING

YOU

You've waited for this moment. Waited for her to look at you and see. Even now, confusion is warring with disbelief on her face. She doesn't understand why you shot Michael. She doesn't understand who you are or what she is to you.

But Dean does. You see the exact moment that everything falls into place for the boy you trained. The lessons you taught them, the little hints you dropped along the way. The way you are with Cassie, grooming her in your own image. The resemblance between the two of you.

Your hair is red, too.

Dean aims his gun at you, but you're not frightened. You've seen inside this boy's head. You know exactly what to say, exactly how to play him. You're the one who told him to bring the gun. You're the one who made sure that no one knew that he and Cassie were leaving the house. You're the one who brought them here.

It's all part of the plan—and Dean is just one more body, one more thing standing between you and your heart's desire.

Cassie. Lorelai's daughter.

You told her not to do anything stupid. She and Dean were supposed to come alone.

You're going to have to punish her for that.

gent Locke was holding a gun. She'd shot Michael—
she'd *shot him*—and now he was on the ground,
blood pooling around his body, his insides leaking
out. This was a mistake—it had to be a mistake. She'd seen
that he was holding a weapon and she'd reacted. She was an
FBI agent, and she wanted to protect me. That was her job.

"Cassie." Dean's voice was low and full of warning. The
set of his features made him look like a predator, a soldier, a
machine. "Stay back."

"No," Agent Locke said, moving forward, smiling as
brightly as ever. "Don't stay back. Don't listen to him, Cassie."

Dean tracked her movement with the gun. His finger
bore down on the trigger.

"Are you a killer, Dean?" Agent Locke asked, her eyes
wide and earnest. "We always wondered. Director Sterling

was hesitant to fund the program, because he knows where you came from. *What* you came from. Is it really fair of us to teach you everything there is to know about killers? To force you to live in a house where their pictures line the walls and everything you see and do is geared toward that one thing? Given your background, how long could it possibly be until you snap?"

Agent Locke was closer to him now. "It's what you think about. It's your greatest fear. How long," Agent Locke drawled, "until you're just . . . like . . . Daddy?"

Arms steady, eyes hard, Dean pulled the trigger, but he was too late. She was on him. She knocked the gun to the side, and when it went off, the bullet flew astray, so close to my face that I could feel the heat of it against my skin. Dean turned his head to look at me, to make sure that I was okay. It cost him a fraction of a second, but even that was too much.

Agent Locke hit him with the butt of her gun, and he went down, his body limp, his crumpled form lying three feet away from Michael's.

"Finally," Agent Locke said, turning around to face me, "it's just us girls."

I took a step forward, toward Michael, toward Dean, but Agent Locke waved her gun at me. "Nuh-uh-uh," she said, making a *tsk*ing sound under her breath. "You stay right there. We're going to have to have a little talk about following orders. I told you not to do anything stupid. Letting Michael trail you here was stupid. It was *sloppy.*"

One second she was standing there, looking exactly like the woman I knew, full of life, a force of nature who was very good at getting her own way, and the next she was on top of me. I saw a blur of silver and heard the impact of her gun with my cheekbone.

Pain exploded in my face a second later. I was on the floor. I could taste blood in my mouth.

"Stand up." Her voice was brisk, but there was an edge to it I'd never heard before. *"Stand up."*

I clambered to my feet. She took her left hand and placed her fingers under my chin. She angled my face upward. There was blood on my lips. I could feel my eye swelling shut, and even the slight movement of my head sent stars into my eyes.

"I told you not to do anything stupid. I told you I'd make you regret it if you did." Her fingernails dug into the skin under my chin, and I thought about the victims' photos, the way she'd peeled the skin from their faces.

The knife.

"Don't do anything else that I'll be forced to make you regret," she said coldly. "You'll only be hurting yourself."

I looked into her eyes, and I wondered how I could have missed this, how I could have spent all day, every day with her for weeks without realizing that there was something wrong with her.

"Why?" I should have kept my mouth shut. I should have been looking for a way out, but there wasn't one, and I needed to know.

Locke ignored my question and glanced at Michael. "It's a pity," she said. "I'd hoped to spare him. He has a very valuable gift, and he certainly took a shine to you. They all did."

With no warning whatsoever, she hit me again. This time, she caught me before I fell.

"You're just like your mother," she said. And then she tightened her grip on my arm, forcing me to stand straight. "Don't be weak. You're better than that. *We're* better than that, and I won't have you sniveling on the floor like some common whore. Do you understand me?"

I understood that the words she was saying were things that someone had probably once said to her. I understood that if I asked her how she knew my mother, she'd hit me again and again.

I understood that I might not get back up.

"I expect an answer when I talk to you, Cassie. You weren't raised in a barn."

"I understand," I said, filing away her choice of words, the almost maternal undertone to her words. I'd assumed that the UNSUB was male. I'd assumed that when the UNSUB killed females, there might be some kind of underlying sexual motivation. But Agent Locke was the one who'd taught me that when you changed one assumption, you changed everything.

You'll always be wrong about something. You'll always miss something. What if the UNSUB is older than you thought? What if he is a she?

She'd practically told me that she was the UNSUB, and it had gone right over my head, because I'd trusted her, because if the UNSUB's motivation wasn't sexual, if he wasn't killing his wife or his mother or a girl who turned him down, over and over again, if *he* was a *she* . . .

"Okay, kiddo, let's get this show on the road." Locke sounded so much like herself, so normal, that it was hard to remember she was holding a gun. "I've got a present for you. I'm going to go get it. If you move while I'm gone, if you so much as blink, I'll put a bullet in your knee, beat you within an inch of your life, and put a matching bullet in lover boy's head."

She gestured toward Dean. He was unconscious, but alive. And Michael . . .

I couldn't even look at Michael's body, lying prone on the floor.

"I won't move."

She was only gone for seconds. I took a single step toward Michael's abandoned gun and froze, because I knew our captor was telling the truth. She'd kill Dean. She'd hurt me.

Even a moment's hesitation was too long, and an instant later, Locke was back—and she wasn't alone.

"Please don't hurt me. Please. My dad has money. He'll give you whatever you want, just please don't—"

It took me a moment to recognize Genevieve Ridgerton. There were ugly cuts on her neck and shoulders. Her face was swollen beyond recognition, and there was blood crusted on her scalp. The skin around her mouth was pink, like someone had just ripped off a strip of tape. She made a mewling sound, halfway between a gargle of water and a moan.

"I told you once," Agent Locke said to me, knife in hand and a wide smile growing on her face, "that I was only ever a Natural at one thing."

I struggled to remember the exchange, one of the first things she'd ever said to me, a mischievous gleam in her eyes. I'd assumed she was referring to sex—but the helpless, hopeless expression in Genevieve's eyes left very little doubt what Locke's so-called gift was.

Torture.

Mutilation.

Death.

She considered herself a Natural killer, and she was waiting for me to say something. Waiting for me to compliment her work.

You knew my mother. You hit me, you hurt me, you told me

it was my fault. You were almost certainly abused as a child. You called me kiddo. *I'm not like your other victims. You sent me presents. You groomed me.*

"The first day we met," I said, hoping the expression on my face looked earnest enough, innocent enough to please her, "when you said you were a Natural at only one thing, you also said that you couldn't tell me about it until I was twenty-one."

Locke looked genuinely pleased that I remembered. "That was before I knew you," she said. "Before I realized how very like me you were. I knew you were Lorelai's daughter. Of course I knew—I was the one who flagged you in the system. I spoon-fed you to Briggs. I brought you here, because you were Lorelai's, but once I started working with you . . ." Her eyes were alight with a strange glow, like a blushing bride's or a pregnant lady's, brimming with happiness from the inside out. "You were mine, Cassie. You belonged with me. I thought I could wait until you were older, until you were ready, but you're ready *now.*"

She pushed Genevieve roughly down to her knees. The girl collapsed, her body shaking, the taste of her terror potent in the air. Locke saw me looking at Genevieve, and she smiled.

"I got her for you."

Gun still in her right hand, Locke held her knife out to

me with her left, hilt first. The look in her eyes was hopeful, vulnerable, *hungry*.

You want something from me.

Locke didn't want to kill me—or maybe she did, but she wanted this more. She wanted me to take the knife. She wanted me to slit Genevieve's throat. She wanted me to be her protégé in more ways than one.

"Take the knife."

I took the knife. I eyed the gun, still in her hands, trained on my forehead.

"Is that really necessary?" I asked, trying to act as though the thought of turning this knife against the sobbing girl on the floor didn't make me want to throw up. "If I'm going to do this, I want it to be *mine*."

I was speaking her language, telling her what she wanted to hear: that I was like *her*, that we were the *same*, that I understood that this was about anger and control and having the power to decide who lived and who died. Slowly, Locke lowered the gun, but she didn't put it down. I measured the distance between us, wondering if I could sink the knife into her before she could get a shot off at me.

She was stronger than I was. She was better trained. She was a killer.

Stalling for time, I knelt next to Genevieve. I bent down, bringing my lips to her ear, letting the expression on my face take on a hint of the madness I saw in Locke's. Then, my voice so low that only Genevieve could hear me, I whispered to the girl, "I'm not going to hurt you. I'm going to get you out of here."

Genevieve looked up, her body still crumpled into a ball on the floor. She reached out and grabbed me by the front of my shirt.

"Kill me," she pleaded, the words escaping cracked and bleeding lips. "You kill me, before she does."

I knelt there, frozen, and Locke lost it. She morphed from a teacher observing her star pupil into an angry, animal creature. She pounced on Genevieve, turning the girl on her back, pinning her to the floor, her hands encircling her neck.

"You don't touch Cassie," she said, her voice rising to a yell, her face so close to Genevieve's that the younger girl had nowhere to go. "You. Don't. Get. To. Decide."

My brain whirred. I had to get her off Genevieve. I had to stop her. I had to—

One second Locke was on Genevieve, and the next she ripped the knife out of my hand.

"You can't do it," she spat at me. "You can't do *anything* right."

Genevieve opened her mouth. Locke plunged the knife into her side. I'd promised to protect Genevieve, and now . . .

Now, there was blood.

CHAPTER 37

ocke stood up. She kicked Genevieve's body to the side, like the girl was already dead, even though the gasping, whimpering sounds the dying girl made told me she was not. Locke's gun was on the floor, forgotten, but the way she was holding the knife as she stepped toward me told me that I wasn't any safer than I'd been a moment before.

She was going to cut me.

She was going to slice me open.

She was going to kill me.

"You're a liar," she said. "You couldn't do it. Do you even want to? Do you?"

She was screaming now. I took a step backward. I opened my mouth to tell her what she wanted to hear, to tell her that I did want it, to stall for time, but she never gave me the chance. Looking at me over the blade, she took another step forward.

"You were supposed to kill her," she said. "I got her for *you*."

"I'm sorry—"

"'Sorry' never did anything! *Lorelai* was sorry. She was sorry, but she had to go, and she left me there alone." Locke's voice broke, but the fury was still clear in every word. "You were supposed to kill the girl. It was supposed to be *us*, Cassie. You. And me. But *you left!*"

She wasn't talking to me anymore. She didn't see *me* when her wild eyes landed on mine. The blade in her hand gleamed. The blood dripped onto the floor. I had two seconds, maybe three.

"What do you mean, I left?" I asked, hoping my words would break through the fog in her brain, bring her back to the here and now. "Left where?"

Locke stopped. She hesitated. She looked at me. She saw me. She got ahold of herself, and with her voice still full of venom, she advanced. "Lorelai left. She was eighteen, and I was twelve. She was supposed to protect me. She was supposed to watch out for me. At night, when Daddy went away and the monster came out to play, she made him angry. She made him angry on purpose so he'd hit her instead of me. She said she wouldn't let anything happen to me." Locke paused. "She lied."

We'd known that the UNSUB was fixated on my mother. We just hadn't known why.

"She was my sister, and she just left me there. She knew what he was like after Mama left. She knew what he would do to me once she was gone, and she left anyway. Because of *you*. Because Daddy was right, and Lorelai was a little whore. She did all the wrong things, and when I found out she was pregnant with that air force boy's baby . . ." Locke was completely caught up in the memory. I eyed her gun on the floor, wondering if I could reach it in time. "I thought that Daddy would kill her if he knew. *I* wasn't even supposed to know, but I found out, and he found out, and he wasn't even angry! He didn't slit her throat, didn't carve up her pretty little face until the boys didn't want her anymore. She was pregnant, and he was happy.

"And then she left. In the middle of the night. She woke me up, and she kissed me, and she told me she was leaving. She told me she wasn't ever coming back, that she wouldn't raise a baby in this house, that our daddy wouldn't ever lay a finger on *you*." Locke's knuckles—my aunt's knuckles—tightened around the base of the blade. Her hand shook. "I begged her to take me with her, but she said she couldn't. That he'd come after us. That she didn't have any legal right to take me. That it would be *too hard*. She left me there to rot, and once she was gone, the only person left for him to punish was me."

Don't do anything else that I'll be forced to make you regret. You'll only be hurting yourself.

I won't have you sniveling on the floor like a common whore.

My mother had never talked about her family. She'd never mentioned an abusive father or an absent mother. She'd never mentioned a little sister, but now I could *see* their family unit: the bruises and the welts and the terror, the Daddy-monster, the little sister that she couldn't save, and the baby that she could.

"When people ask me why I do what I do," the woman who was that baby sister said, "I tell them that I went into the FBI because a loved one was murdered. I'd finally gotten out of that house. I went to college, and I spent years looking for my big sister. At first, I just wanted to find her. I just wanted to be with her—and with you. If she'd taken me with you, I could have helped! You would have loved me. I would have loved you." Locke's voice got very soft, and I realized that this was a scenario she'd played out in her head, growing up in that hellhole. She'd thought about my mom, and she'd thought about me before she ever met me, before she ever knew my name.

"She shouldn't have left you there." I braved saying the words because they felt true. Locke was just a kid when my mother left, and my mom had never even looked back. She'd raised me on the road, moving from city to city, never letting it slip that she had a family out there, just like she'd never mentioned my dad.

My whole life, we'd been running from something, and I didn't even know it.

"She never should have left me there," Locke repeated. "Eventually, I stopped dreaming about finding her and being a family again, and I started dreaming about finding her and hurting her, the way Daddy hurt me. Making her pay for leaving me there. Peeling her face off until no one thought she was the pretty one, until just looking at her made *you* scream."

The dressing room. The blood. The smell . . .

"But by the time I found her—by the time I found you— it was too late. She was already dead. She was gone, and it wasn't fair. *I* was supposed to kill her. *I* was supposed to be the one."

My aunt hadn't killed my mother—because someone else had gotten there first.

"When I found out that she was dead, and you were gone, when I found out that they'd sent you to live with your *father's* family—I was your family, too! I thought about taking you. I even went to Colorado, but when I got there, there was this junkie at my motel. She was cheap and loose and dirty, and her hair was the exact right shade of red. I killed her, and I said, 'How do you like that, Lore?' I carved her up until I could imagine Lorelai's face underneath, and God, it felt good." She paused. "It was the sweetest, you know. The first time. It always is. And after the first time, you always need more."

"Is that why you joined the FBI?" I asked. "Lots of travel, easy access, the perfect cover?"

Agent Locke took a step toward me. Every muscle in her body was taut. For a moment, I thought that she would hit me—again and again and again.

"No," she said. "That's not why I joined."

When people ask me why I do what I do, I tell them that I went into the FBI because a loved one was murdered.

Locke's words came back to me then, and I realized that she'd been telling the truth.

"You joined the FBI because you wanted to find my mother's killer."

Not because she was upset that my mom was dead. Because she'd wanted to be the one to kill her.

"I changed my name. I studied. I planned. I passed the psych exams with flying colors. Even once Briggs and I started working together and he brought me in on the Naturals program, no one really saw me. They only saw what I wanted them to see. Lia never caught me in a lie. Michael never saw a hint of unsavory emotion. And Dean— I was like family to him."

Hearing Dean's name made my eyes dart over to his body. He still wasn't moving—but Michael was. His eyes were open. He was bleeding. He couldn't walk, he couldn't even crawl, but he was pulling himself slowly across the floor—to his gun.

Locke moved to follow my gaze, but I stopped her.

"It isn't the same," I said, my voice decisive and calm.

"What isn't?" Locke—no, her name wasn't really Locke, not if she was my mother's sister—said.

I had less than a second to think of an answer, but growing up the daughter of a woman who made her living by pretending to be psychic hadn't just taught me the BPEs. For better or worse, I'd learned to put on a show, so I said the one thing I could think of that would keep Lacey *Hobbes's* attention focused solely and 100 percent on me.

"You tried to restage my mother's murder, but you got it wrong. What you're doing to these women isn't the same as what *I* did to my mother."

The woman in front of me had wanted to kill my mother, but she'd also desperately wanted her acceptance. She'd wanted to be a part of a family, and she'd brought me here tonight with some twisted hope that I could be that for her. She'd enjoyed being my mentor. She wanted me to be like her.

Now my job was to convince her that I was.

"My mother didn't protect you," I said, mirroring the rage and desperation and hurt I saw on her face. "She didn't protect me, either. There were men. She didn't love them. She didn't stay with them. She didn't say a word when they took their frustrations out on me. She was weak. She was a whore. She *hurt* me."

Lia would have known I was lying, but the woman in front of me wasn't Lia. I smiled, letting the expression spread slowly across my face, keeping my eyes on my aunt, never looking, even for a second, at Michael.

"So I hurt her."

My aunt stared at me, her face still twisted in disbelief, but her eyes wistful with longing.

"She was getting ready. Putting on her lipstick. Pretending she was so perfect and so special, that she wasn't a monster. I said her name. She turned around, and I took my knife. I plunged it into her stomach. She said my name. That was it. Just 'Cassie.' So I stabbed her again. And again. She fought. She kicked and she screamed, but this time, I was the one with the power. I was the one doing the hurting, and she was the one getting hurt. She fell on her stomach. I flipped her over so I could see her face. I didn't drag the knife over her cheekbones. I didn't carve her up. I dipped my fingers into her side. I made her scream. And then I painted her lips with blood."

Locke—no, Hobbes—*Lacey* was captivated. For a single second, I thought she might believe me. Her knife hand hung loosely by her side. Her other hand reached into her pocket. She pulled something out—I couldn't see what. She fingered it for a moment—gingerly, carefully—and then she crushed her fingers into a fist.

"An excellent performance," she said. "But I'm a profiler, too. I've been doing this a lot longer than you have, Cassie, and your mother wasn't killed by a twelve-year-old girl. You're not a killer. You don't have what it takes." She lifted the knife and started forward, the longing in her eyes turning to something else.

Bloodlust.

"You're not going to get away with this," I said, dropping the act as she advanced on me. "They'll know it was you. They'll catch you—"

"No," Locke corrected. "*I'll* catch Dean. You called me from his phone. I was worried, but when I called the house, you weren't there. Everyone went into an uproar. They found out Dean was missing, too, and that he'd stolen Briggs's guns. I tracked you down. I found Dean here with Genevieve. *He* shot Michael. *He* carved you up. I'm the heroic agent who stopped him, who figured out that the DC murders were the work of a copycat with access to our system, unrelated to the other murders altogether. I was too late to save you, but I did manage to kill Dean before he could kill me. Like father, like son.

"Did you really think you could win?" she asked. "Did you think you could fool me?"

Behind her, Michael had the gun in his hand. He rolled onto his side. He aimed.

"I never expected you to believe me," I said. "Or to let me live. I just needed you to listen."

Her eyes met mine. They widened. A gunshot went off. Then two, then three, four, five. And my aunt Lacey fell to the floor, her body splayed out next to Genevieve.

Dead.

PART FIVE:
DECIDING

CHAPTER 38

Michael was in the hospital for two weeks. Dean was released after two days. But even once we were back at the house, even once the case was closed, none of us had really recovered.

Genevieve Ridgerton had survived—barely. She'd refused to see any of us—especially me.

Michael had months of physical rehabilitation ahead of him. The doctors said he might never walk without a limp again. Dean had barely said a word to me. Sloane couldn't talk about anything other than the absolute unlikelihood of a serial killer being able to pass the psych evals and background check necessary to join the FBI, even under an assumed name. And I was dealing with the fact that Lacey Locke, née Hobbes, was my aunt.

Her story had checked out. She and my mother were born and raised outside of Baton Rouge, though both had shed their accents along the way. Their father, Clayton Hobbes, had been convicted twice of assault and battery—once against his wife, who ran off when my mother was nine and Lacey was three. The girls had attended school until the ages of ten and sixteen, but the system had lost them somewhere along the way.

They'd grown up in hell. My mother had gotten out. Lacey hadn't.

The Bureau cross-referenced Lacey's murders with cases that Briggs's team had worked, and they discovered at least five more that fit the pattern. The agents would fly out on a case; Lacey would slip away, and somewhere, forty or fifty miles away, someone would disappear. They would die. And if a police report was filed, it never made its way to the FBI's attention, because the crime didn't appear to be serial in nature.

The woman who'd called herself Lacey Locke had paid attention to state lines. She'd never killed in the same state twice—until I joined the Naturals program. She'd escalated then, committing a series of murders here in DC as she became increasingly fixated on me.

At least fourteen people were dead, and a senator's daughter had been kidnapped and gravely injured. The case was a nightmare for the Bureau—and a nightmare for us. The prohibition against Naturals' participation in active cases was back and stronger than ever. Director Sterling had managed to keep our names out of the news this time. As far as he was concerned, all anyone needed to know was that the killer was dead.

My aunt was dead.

Just like my mother.

Two weeks after Michael had pulled the trigger, I could still see those last moments playing out, over and over again. I sat beside the pool, dangling my feet in the water and wondering what happened next.

Where did I go from here?

"If you're going to leave the program, leave. But for God's sake, Cassie, if you're going to stay, stop moping around like your kitty cat has cancer, and do something about it."

I turned to see Lia standing above me. She was the one person who hadn't changed as a result of all of this. In a way, it was almost comforting to know that I could count on her to stay the same.

"What do you want me to do?" I asked, pulling my feet out of the pool and standing up so that we were eye to eye.

"You can start by getting rid of that Rose Red lipstick I gave you," Lia said. Leave it to her to know that I still had it, that I'd carried the tube she'd given me everywhere I went since discovering an ancient tube of Rose Red, worn to a nub, in my aunt's hand the night she died. Apparently, it had been my mother's color of choice even as a girl. Lacey had kept it all these years.

That was what she'd carried in her pocket.

That was what she'd held as I'd spun my story about my mother's death.

The FBI had found a dozen other lipsticks in a cabinet at her house. Keepsakes that she took from each victim. A little sister, dying to be like big sis, stealing her lipstick until the end.

She was the one who'd given the makeup to Lia. She'd bought a fresh tube of Rose Red just for me, and Lia had played right into her hands. Now that it was over, I should have thrown the lipstick away, but I couldn't seem to bring myself to do it. It was a reminder: of the things my aunt had done, of what I'd survived, of my mother and the fact that Lacey and I had both joined the FBI in hopes of finding her killer.

A killer who was still out there. A killer who not even a psychotic, obsessive FBI agent had been able to find. Since joining the program, I'd gained and lost a mentor and seen my mother's only other living relative shot dead. I'd helped take down a killer who'd been re-creating my mother's death for years—but I was still no closer to finding the monster who'd actually killed her. I might never get answers.

They might never find her body.

"Well?" Lia had done a good impression of a patient person, but clearly, her capacity for waiting for me to reply had been stretched to its limit and then some. "Are you in or are you out?"

"I'm not going anywhere," I said. "I'm in this, but I'm keeping the lipstick."

"Rawrrrrr." Lia made a scratching motion. "Somebody's finally growing claws."

"Yeah," I said dryly. "I love you, too."

I turned around to walk into the house, but Lia's voice stopped me halfway there.

"I'm not saying I like you. I'm not saying I'm going to stop eating your ice cream or stealing your clothes, and I'm certainly not saying that I won't make your life a living nightmare if you jerk Dean around, but I wouldn't want you to leave." Lia strode past me, then turned around and flashed me a smile. "You make things interesting. And besides, I'm kind of into the idea of Michael's war wounds, and having my way with him will be that much sweeter knowing you're right down the hall."

Lia flounced back into the house. I thought of the scars Michael would have once he'd healed, thought of the kiss, the fact that he'd almost died for me—and then I thought of Dean.

Dean, who hadn't forgiven himself for not being able to pull the trigger.

Dean, whose father was as much of a monster as my aunt.

Weeks ago, Lia had told me that every person in this house was fundamentally screwed up to the depths of our dark and shadowy souls. We all had our crosses to bear. We saw things that other people didn't—things that people our age should never have to see.

Dean would never just be a boy. He'd always be the serial killer's son. Michael would always be the person who'd put a round of bullets in my aunt. And part of me would never leave my mother's blood-soaked dressing room, just like another part would always be at the safe house, with Lacey and her knife.

We would never be like other people.

"I don't know what the back door did to you," an amused voice told me, "but I'm sure it's really, truly sorry."

Michael was supposed to be using a wheelchair, but he was already trying to maneuver on crutches—an impossible feat, considering a bullet had also been lodged in his shoulder.

"I'm not glaring at the back door," I said.

Michael raised one eyebrow, higher and higher until I caved.

"Fine," I said. "I might have been glaring at the back door. I don't want to talk about it."

"Like you didn't want to talk about that kiss?" Michael's voice was light, but this was the first time either of us had brought up that moment in my bedroom.

"Michael—"

"Don't." He stopped me. "If I hadn't been so jealous of Dean, I wouldn't have bought your little story for a second. Even as it was, I didn't buy it for much longer than that."

"You came after me," I said.

"I'll always come after you," he said, wiggling his eyebrows in a way that made the words seem like more of a joke than a promise.

Something told me it was both.

"But you and Redding have something. I don't know what it is. I don't blame you for it." On crutches, he couldn't lean toward me. He couldn't reach out and brush the hair out of my face. But something about the curve of his lips was more intimate than any touch. "A lot has happened. You have a lot to figure out. I can be a patient man, Colorado. A devastatingly handsome, roguishly scarred, heartbreakingly courageous, patient man."

I rolled my eyes, but couldn't bite back a smile.

"So take whatever time you need. Figure out how you feel. Figure out if Dean makes you feel the way I do, if he'll ever let you in, and if you want him to, because the next time my lips touch yours, the next time your hands are buried in my hair—the only person you're going to be thinking about is me."

I stood there, looking at Michael and wondering how it was possible that I could instinctively understand other people—*their* personalities, *their* beliefs, *their* desires—but that when it came to what *I* wanted, I was just like anyone else, muddled and confused and stumbling through.

I didn't know what it meant that my aunt had been a killer, or how I felt about the fact that she was dead.

I didn't know who had killed my mother, or what losing her and never getting any closure had done to me. I didn't know if I was capable of really letting someone else in. I didn't know if I could fall in love.

I didn't know what I wanted or who I wanted to be with.

But standing there, looking at Michael, the one thing I did know, the way I always knew things about other people, was that sooner or later, as a part of this program—a part of this *team*—I was going to find out.

ACKNOWLEDGMENTS

T*he Naturals* might be the most challenging and rewarding book I've ever written. I'm grateful to have had the opportunity to combine my love of psychology and knowledge of cognitive science with my passion for YA, and I owe a major debt of gratitude to the many people who helped me along the way.

Major thanks go to my editor, Catherine Onder, whose passion for this project and keen eye helped me make this a book I couldn't have written on my own. My agent, Elizabeth Harding, has been with me every step of the way for a dozen books now, and I feel continually lucky to have her on my side. My UK agent, Ginger Clark, and everyone at Quercus Books have been such supporters of this project from its conception—I'm so grateful to have such tremendous teams behind the book on both sides of the pond. And, of course,

I owe huge thank-you's to everyone at Disney-Hyperion, including Dina Sherman (for—among other things—two-stepping!). Thanks, too, to my film agent, Holly Frederick, and to Lorenzo De Maio for asking questions that made me go further into this world.

Writing this book involved a lot of research. I owe particular debts to the memoirs of FBI profiler John Douglas, and to the empirical research of Paul Ekman, Maureen O'Sullivan, Simon Baron-Cohen, and many others.

As a writer—and a person—I've been blessed with an incredible support system, and I've never relied on it as much for my own sanity as I did in the writing and editing of this book. A big thank-you to Ally Carter, BFF extraordinaire, for talking me down off many a cliff and for reading an earlier draft of this book. Thanks also to Sarah Cross, Sarah Rees Brennan, Melissa Marr, Rachel Vincent, BOB, and so many others for their friendship and support through the ups and downs of publishing and the creative process.

The writing and revising of this book spanned the last year of my PhD and my first year as a college professor. Thank you to my cohorts and advisors at Yale, and to everyone in the psychology department at the University of Oklahoma for being so welcoming my first year as a professor there—and so supportive of my books! I'd also like to thank my incredible students, especially those in my Cognitive Science of Fiction and Writing Young Adult Fiction classes last spring.

Teaching you has been such an amazing experience, and I'm a better writer for it!

Finally, thanks—as always—go to my incredible family. Mom, Dad, Justin, Allison, and Connor, I love you more than words can say.